LOVE ME LIKE THIS

The Morrisons, Book 3

Justin & Taylor

Bella Andre

LOVE ME LIKE THIS

The Morrisons, Book 3

Justin & Taylor

© Bella Andre 2018

Sign up for Bella's New Release Newsletter

www.BellaAndre.com/newsletter

bella@bellaandre.com

www.BellaAndre.com

Bella on Twitter: @bellaandre

Bella on Facebook: facebook.com/bellaandrefans

Eight years have passed since Justin Morrison first laid eyes on Taylor Cardenes and fell head over heels in love with her, even though he knew she could never be his. He's tried everything he can to get over her—including moving to another country—but she's still the only woman he'll ever want.

Eight years is a heck of a long time to secretly love someone. Taylor knows all too well how impossible it is to forget a man as sexy, sweet, and brilliant as Justin Morrison. So when he turns up on the doorstep of her Napa Valley bed and breakfast, she longs for the happily-ever-after of her dreams.

As Taylor and Justin spend beautifully romantic mornings together watching the sun rise over the vineyards—and can't help but fall into each other's arms on wickedly sexy nights—it looks like they might finally get their chance at the love they've been waiting for. But will the secret Taylor has been keeping shatter everything in the end?

Note from Bella

As soon as I began to write about the Morrison family several years ago, I fell in love with them. Thankfully, after receiving countless emails and notes on Facebook and Twitter from readers telling me how much you loved *Kiss Me Like This* and *Tempt Me Like This*, I knew I wasn't alone. But the truth is that I had no idea just how deep my attachment to the Morrisons would go until I finally got a chance to tell Justin and Taylor's story.

Every day, I write about heroes and heroines who are utterly devoted to each other, so it's not uncommon for my husband to find me sitting at my laptop with tears rolling down my cheeks as I write a particularly poignant scene. But I'm pretty sure I broke a record for the most teary-eyed writing days while working on *Love Me Like This*.

I hope you absolutely adore reading about Justin and Taylor's long awaited happily ever after.

Happy reading,
Bella Andre

P.S. If you would like to hear about my new books as soon as they're released, please sign up for my New Release newsletter: BellaAndre.com/Newsletter

CHAPTER ONE

"You've booked a vacation for me in Napa Valley?" Justin Morrison was sitting with his sisters Olivia and Madison at the kitchen table in their childhood home in Palo Alto as they sprang this surprise on him. "I thought you needed me here a week early to help get all the last-minute things done for Drew and Ashley's wedding." If that hadn't been the case, he likely wouldn't have left his lab in Frankfurt until a day or two before the wedding to catch a plane to SFO. Of course, he was happy his brother was getting married to the woman of his dreams, but Justin could barely squeeze one free hour out of his research schedule, let alone an entire week.

He thought he saw a flash of guilt in Olivia's eyes, but a split second later, it was gone. "As you know, Ashley is really organized, so it turns out she doesn't need much help with anything. Which means," Olivia added with a smile that he didn't quite buy, "you're free to take a little holiday before the wedding."

"Apart from a few days at Thanksgiving and Christmas, I've barely been home for the past five years," he reminded her. "And now that I've got a free week to spend with everyone, you're trying to get rid of me?"

"Of course not." Maddie was quick to throw her arms around him to back up her words.

He couldn't believe how grown up his little sister was. When he'd left for Germany five years ago, she'd been a sweet, naïve eighteen-year-old. Now, at twenty-three, while she still had that same joyful smile, Justin was all too certain that her naïve years were long behind her. His jaw clenched at the thought of his little sister getting involved with some scumbag—which would be *all* guys as far as he was concerned. He'd been planning to pin her down on everything this week, from her love life to her cooking career, but now it looked as though she was trying to get rid of him instead.

As she loosened her hold on him, he was struck by the concern in her eyes. "We're worried about you, Justin."

"Worried?" He looked between Maddie and Olivia. "Why would you be worried about me?"

Olivia's lips pressed together as she gathered her thoughts. He'd seen this look many times, especially after their mother had passed away six years ago from breast cancer and Olivia had done her best to step into their mom's shoes. Not even his brilliant sister could manage that, however. Lisa Morrison was irreplaceable, and he felt her loss just as keenly today as he had all those years ago. Losing his mother had driven Justin to find a cure for breast cancer—and he wouldn't rest until he did.

"You work too hard." Olivia's words were soft but firm.

"You're kidding, right?" He couldn't believe Olivia, of all people, was accusing him of being a workaholic. She was in her last year of a PhD program in education, the same field their mother had worked in, teaching third grade. Last time Justin had been home for Thanksgiving, Olivia's nose had been buried in research papers for two days straight—she'd barely put her work down to eat some stuffing. "When was the last time *you* saw the sun?"

"Actually," Olivia said, straightening her shoulders and lifting her chin, "I've been cutting back a lot recently."

When a flush moved across her cheeks, he suddenly wondered if he'd been planning to quiz the wrong sister about her love life. Olivia was twenty-eight, so he shouldn't be surprised that she might have met someone she was interested in going the distance with. If she had, was there any chance in hell that the guy was good enough for her? All the more reason for Justin to spend the week here in Palo Alto with his family instead of in the wine country.

"In any case, we're not talking about me," she continued in a brisk tone. "We're talking about you. A week in a charming B&B surrounded by the beautiful vineyards of St. Helena is exactly what you need."

He ran his hand through his hair, still trying to figure out what was behind their decision to surprise him with this trip. "Does Grant know about this?"

Maddie and Olivia both nodded as his younger sister told him, "Grant is the one who made the booking."

Now Justin was *really* confused. His oldest brother ran Collide, a social networking company that now also included venture capital and a record company, which made Grant quite possibly the hardest worker of them all. Surely he couldn't think Justin was working too hard in the lab—especially when Grant's company was one of the investors with a stake in Justin's research.

"Are Sean and Drew also in on your plan to send me off into the boonies?"

"First of all," Olivia said, "St. Helena is anything but the boonies. It's considered to be one of the best small towns in America. And second, when we ran the idea past Sean and Drew, they both gave it the thumbs-up."

"So all of you have been talking about me behind my back?"

"We just want you to be happy." Maddie grabbed his hands and squeezed them. "Can you trust us, Justin? Please?"

Before he could reply, their dad walked in through the side door. Michael Morrison's face lit up when he saw his kids sitting at the table. "Justin, you're back!"

Twelve or twenty-seven—it didn't matter how old Justin was, he always wanted one of his father's hugs. When the two men embraced, he was glad that his father didn't feel frail or bony anymore. He had never carried excess weight, but when his wife died, he'd gone from being fit and trim to a walking skeleton.

"You're looking good, Dad."

"Thanks." His father put his laptop bag on the white and blue hand-painted tiles that Justin had helped his mother install a decade ago. "I've been playing a lot of pickleball lately. Maybe you could join me for a game this week."

"It will have to be tonight." Olivia sent his father a look. "Justin will be in St. Helena next week, remember?"

"Oh yeah." His father cleared his throat and looked a little nervous as he said, "You're going to have a great time up there. Really, really great!"

Seriously suspicious now, Justin said, "Okay, one of you had better tell me what the heck is going on, and quick."

Olivia shot both his father and Maddie quelling looks. But Justin knew whom to turn to for answers. "Mads?" He leaned over the table and put his face in line with hers. "You know I'm going to get you to tell me everything before the night is through, so you might as well just give up the info now and save us both the trouble."

She scrunched her eyes shut tight, her nose crinkling too, just like she used to when she was a little girl trying to keep a secret. Justin started the silent countdown inside his head: *ten, nine, eight, seven, six*—she always broke by three—*five, four*—

"Taylor." The name burst from her lips.

"Taylor?" Whatever Justin had been expecting to hear, it hadn't been the name of his best friend from college. A friend he'd fallen completely out of touch with during the past five years.

He still remembered the day they'd met—in a bio lab during their first quarter at Stanford University. Taylor was the prettiest girl Justin had ever set eyes on. She hadn't had any makeup on, hadn't worn flashy or revealing clothes the way so many girls from high school had. She'd slain him with nothing more than a sweet, and somewhat shy, smile.

When it turned out she was wicked smart too, he'd angled to be her lab partner—hoping it would mean that they'd spend plenty of time together outside of the lab. Thankfully, they soon became good friends. But their relationship never went any further than that, because she had a boyfriend back home in Rochester, New York.

Boring Bruce, Justin secretly called him. The guy was the son of her parents' best friends, and the two of them had been set up practically from the cradle. She never said much about Bruce to Justin—and he sure as hell hadn't wanted to ask for details about their love life. But from her side of the phone conversations he sometimes overheard, it didn't exactly seem like she was living a fairy-tale romance with the guy.

Still, he'd known better than to say a damn thing about her relationship when his motivations were completely suspect—he would have given his right arm for Taylor to break up with her boyfriend so that he could have her for himself. Especially in junior year, when his mother passed away and Taylor had unequivocally been there for him and his family. She'd been there for his mother too, spending hours upon hours at the hospital, all the way until the end.

By senior year, Justin had run out of patience—and self-control. When Taylor was near, all he could think about was kissing her. Pulling her into his arms and finding out if they were as good together as his fantasies told him they'd be.

He hadn't been a monk in college. He'd gone from one woman to the next—too many women, if he was being honest with himself—in the hopes that one of them would do the impossible and make him forget how much he wanted Taylor. By senior year, however, he'd started funneling his frustration into his work, day in, day out, and late into the night.

That was when the universe had decided it was time to throw him a bone and magic started happening in the lab. The kind of magic that meant someone else might not lose their mom to breast cancer in the future. Or their sister. Or their daughter. Even though he knew it was rare for an undergraduate to get research funding, he'd told his senior advisor about his findings, and his brother Grant, who said he would put feelers out to see if there were any investors interested in his research.

And then, magic finally happened *outside* of the lab too. Justin and Taylor were celebrating making it through a difficult week at school, and somewhere in there, they'd ended up kissing. Idiot that he was, he'd thought their kiss meant everything had changed. He'd thought it meant she was finally going to be *his*.

But in the morning, she'd been horrified and had fumbled all over herself trying to let him down easy.

Saying she'd been drunk, that she couldn't remember what happened at the bar, that she hoped she hadn't ruined their friendship.

She couldn't have made it any clearer—especially in the way she emphasized the word *friendship*—that she wasn't interested.

Heartbreak, Justin understood in that moment, was just a different shade of grief. Guilt wasn't far behind. He knew she'd had too much to drink that night at the bar, but he'd been so desperate to have her that he hadn't listened to his conscience.

Thank God that same morning his brother Grant called with the offer from Frankfurt to open a lab immediately and get to work taking his research to the next level. Twenty-four hours later, Justin was leaving Stanford on a plane to Germany, planning to bury himself in enough work that he forgot everything else.

Especially his unrequited feelings for Taylor.

Five years later, he had succeeded on both fronts. His team at the lab was so close to a breakthrough that he could taste it. And his desperate need for Taylor was nothing more than a distant memory.

At least, he'd thought so, until his family said her name—and sent him tumbling down memory lane.

His father took off his glasses and cleaned them with his shirttail, another of his standard nervous gestures. "Last month, Grant and I went to take a look at the winery Drew and Ashley are getting married in—Marcus and Nicola Sullivan's place—and we ran into Taylor while we were getting a bite to eat in town." He looked slightly apologetic as he added, "She told us she'd recently moved to St. Helena."

Justin knew why his father looked sorry for him. The fact that Taylor hadn't told him this news herself spoke volumes about the sorry state of their friendship.

In his head, Justin still thought of her as she'd been the last time he'd seen her. Beautiful and sweet, even as she apologized for their drunken kiss. But five years had passed since then. She'd taken a position with a biotech firm in Palo Alto after graduation and had been living in a rental house off College Terrace with a couple of roommates. He hadn't actually seen her, though, had always headed back to California for the holidays just as she was leaving for New York to visit her family—and her boyfriend. At first, there had been email, texts, calls. But soon, one month of silence was stretching into three, and then six, between awkward conversations that felt all wrong.

Finally, he saw what was going on—his family was forcing him to do what he should have done a long time ago: apologize to Taylor for being a terrible friend and hopefully set their friendship back to rights. Whatever happened in St. Helena, he wouldn't put either of them in an awkward position again by trying to kiss her, wouldn't let himself hope that she'd suddenly see him in a different light than she had in college. Besides, he was too busy with the lab for a girlfriend, so just-friends was perfect.

"You're right," he said to his family, "I need to see her. It's been way too long."

Maddie threw her arms around his neck. "I'm so glad you agree! And I'm sure Taylor is happy that you're going to be one of the first guests at her B&B, instead of some stranger."

"Wait a minute." Justin reeled from yet more new information. "*Taylor* owns the B&B you've booked me into?"

Olivia was smiling as she handed him the flyer for the Cardenes Wine Country B&B. "Check-in is at three p.m. The florist that Mom always used is still on University Avenue if you want to pick up some flowers before you head to Napa."

His sister was never one for subtlety. Clearly, she knew he needed to grovel, and she was trying to give him pointers. But he already knew exactly what to bring for Taylor when he saw her tomorrow. Something he'd never had the nerve to give her back in college, but that would hopefully prove to both of them that he could be her friend—and nothing more—without putting pressure on her to change her mind or make her feel as though he blamed her for not loving him back.

"Now that that's settled," his conflict-averse father

said, "how about all of us grab some pickleball racquets and get in a match before dark?"

Heading outside with his family was just what Justin needed. Not only to help with the jet lag, but because he'd soon be seeing Taylor again. And not just for a few hours, but for several days. Without his lab to disappear into, he didn't want to fall into old patterns and start mooning over her again.

"I'm game," he said.

"I am too," Maddie agreed. She flexed her biceps and added, "Just as long as you're not too upset when I crush you on the court."

All the Morrison men were built the same—tall and rangy, with well-defined muscles. Despite his insane work hours, Justin was still fit. Working out was the best way he had to blow off steam and frustration. But to make his sister laugh, he pretended to limp out of the kitchen toward the garage to get the paddles and balls.

And as the four of them played a cutthroat game of pickleball, he realized just how much he'd missed his family's laughter during the past five years. Although the truth was that the laughter had died before that, when his mom got sick.

It was why Justin worked so hard in his lab. So that other families wouldn't forget how to laugh the way they had.

CHAPTER TWO

Nervous wasn't nearly big enough a word for what Taylor Cardenes was feeling. She was opening her B&B to the public today.

And she was finally going to see Justin Morrison again.

She took a deep breath as she turned to look at the building and garden her grandfather had left to her so unexpectedly. Six months ago, her parents had called with the very sad news that her grandfather had passed away in his sleep. Sam Cardenes had been a farmer all his life, growing berries and lemons and nuts, but when Taylor's grandmother had passed away in her early sixties, he'd sold off the farm and retired to St. Helena.

Taylor remembered the first time she'd seen this place. The half-acre garden had been wild and unruly, the rambling Victorian house had needed a new roof…and she'd fallen head over heels in love.

Given her aptitude for science and math, she'd been encouraged to focus on STEM—Science, Technology, Engineering and Math—classes. And she enjoyed thinking through difficult problems in her classes and labs. But she'd never felt anywhere near as at home in a classroom or laboratory as she did in her grandpa's home and garden.

It wasn't something she'd ever admitted out loud, though, not even to her grandfather. But he must have known, because while her parents and brother had been bequeathed Sam's stocks and his classic car, he'd left her his home. In any case, no one else in her family would have wanted this property. All they ever saw when they came to visit were the weeds coming through the fence, the broken floorboards on the wraparound porch, and the chipped tiles on the kitchen counter.

Taylor had turned in her resignation at the biotech firm the very next day. It wasn't like she was curing cancer or anything. The company specialized in "dermatological breakthroughs," which was a fancy way of saying they made expensive skin creams for wealthy women. Still, leaving it was the riskiest thing she'd ever done. The *only* risky thing, actually.

Well, apart from that kiss with Justin five years ago.

No. She needed to stop replaying the night she'd thrown herself at him, stop the flush of heat from moving through her at how good the kiss had been— and how embarrassed she'd been the next morning.

Surely he'd forgotten all about it by now and they could leave the past in the past, where it belonged.

Working to shake the memories away, she admired her newly painted sign—*Cardenes Wine Country B&B*—proud to carry on the family name. The business was another risk she hadn't planned on taking, but which now seemed almost inevitable.

When she'd first moved to St. Helena, she'd thrown herself into remodeling the house and cleaning up the garden while living off her savings. After several months, however, she could no longer put off the uninspiring task of looking for another job. It had been pure serendipity that she had found a box of newspaper clippings in the attic, stories about the years her grandfather's home had been a B&B many decades ago. She hadn't ever thought to be a part of the hospitality business, but the idea of reopening a B&B wouldn't let go.

She'd been terrified, but also elated, the day she'd filed for her business license. For someone who had always done what was expected of her, who had always walked the straight and narrow and most especially the *safe*—the freedom she'd experienced these past few months on her own was heady.

She'd wanted to celebrate that day in the town hall. She'd thought immediately of Justin and wished for the millionth time that he could be there with her instead of thousands of miles away—and most of all that they could still be best friends the way they used to be.

That was when Taylor had crumpled at the registrar's desk, fainting from a sudden pain in her side so intense that passing out was her only option.

Taylor had always been healthy, rarely needing anything more than a couple of over-the-counter pain pills, or a dose of antibiotics at worst, to cure whatever ailed her.

It turned out antibiotics wouldn't be cutting it this time.

She'd studied polycystic kidney disease in college. PKD had been on the physiology final, one of a dozen diseases in a textbook. She'd analyzed the PKD case studies to get an A in the class—not to keep herself alive.

Her cell phone rang with her mother's ring tone. She'd called every single day from the time Taylor had left for college until now. Taylor always felt guilty if she didn't pick up, even more so now that she knew how worried her mother was about her health.

"Hi, Mom." Knowing what the questions were sure to be, she preempted them by saying, "Everything is going great for my opening today, and I'm feeling good."

"I just want to make sure you're not working too hard," Caroline said. "I should have flown out to help."

Her parents had not taken the news of her disease

well, to say the least. They were soft-spoken and loving, but in a distinctly careful way. They had their reasons—two years before Taylor was born, her parents had lost a baby daughter to meningitis—so she understood why they were always so intent on keeping her and her brother safe. They'd wanted her to attend the University of Rochester so that she could live at home while going to college. Her boyfriend, Bruce, had wanted that too, given that he was already a freshman there. But her heart was secretly set on Stanford, and when her acceptance came, no one could deny that it was an opportunity of a lifetime. Her parents had reluctantly let her go, but they'd always been anxious about her living on the West Coast and had wanted her to move back home as soon as she'd graduated. One day she hoped they'd understand that she was a California girl at heart.

"Everyone in town has been so helpful," she told her mother, smiling as she thought about the cookies and flowers and bunches of grapes that had been dropped off by her neighbors that morning. The local paper was even running free ads for her B&B for the first month. "You don't need to worry."

"Of course I'm worrying! Your kidneys are already so impaired that even if you're really careful, the chances of your blood pressure spiking, or having cysts grow in your kidneys and burst, or even, God forbid, having an aneurysm—"

"Mom, stop." She took a deep breath to keep her heart from racing at the list of things that could be going wrong inside her own body right this very second. "You know I'm on the waiting list for a transplant. And until then, I'm doing everything the doctor said to do. I'm eating right and drinking enough water and going for walks and getting my kidney function tested on a regular basis." She was also taking a regular dose of over-the-counter drugs for pain management, but she knew better than to mention *that*.

"If only your father or brother or I were a match, honey, you know we'd donate a kidney to you in a heartbeat."

She did know that, but honestly, she was glad that they weren't. Taylor knew she wasn't the only one who felt that way—many people with kidney disease were deeply reticent to ask their loved ones for a kidney donation. Yes, she understood that successful kidney transplants took place every day all over the world. But she still couldn't let go of the what-ifs.

What if something happened to someone she loved while they were in transplant surgery?

Or what if they made it through surgery all right, but then ended up becoming ill down the road when it turned out they actually *did* need their second kidney to live a long and healthy life?

Or what if they gave her a kidney and her body rejected it, making it a pointless sacrifice on their part?

And, of course, she would never wish harm on anyone so that she could get their organ via the deceased-donor program.

But her mother didn't want to hear any of that, so she simply said, "Everything is going to be okay." It was the mantra she'd been repeating ever since the diagnosis, especially after her last round of tests. Her kidney function was below twenty percent—and rapidly decreasing. It was another fact she didn't think it was wise to mention to her mother until she was in a calmer frame of mind.

A car pulled up in front of her newly painted front gate, and the butterflies started dancing around inside her belly again. "I think my first guests have arrived. I've got to go."

"Call if you need anything, anything at all, and I'll be on the first plane out."

"Thanks, Mom. I love you too."

Dropping the phone into her back pocket, Taylor ran her gaze over her home and garden one more time. This was it—the beginning of her new life.

Shoving the rush of fear aside, she turned to open the front gate...and her heart stopped in its tracks. Though she'd known he'd be here soon, it was still a shock to see him again.

Justin Morrison.

The best friend she'd always secretly loved.

CHAPTER THREE

Justin was stunned speechless, and his heart was racing as though he'd just sprinted around a track. All because the girl he'd tried like hell to forget was standing in front of him...and she definitely wasn't a girl anymore.

Taylor had always been long and lean, with warm brown eyes and a cheerful smile. But he could swear she'd never had curves like these in college. And her mouth hadn't been so full, either, had it? Or her gaze so full of innate sensuality?

He swallowed hard, belatedly realizing he was standing there staring at her like an idiot. He'd planned what he was going to say during the drive, but none of his grand apologies sounded right anymore.

"Taylor." He couldn't keep the emotion from his voice as he said her name. "It's been way too long."

The next thing he knew, she was running into his arms and he was holding her the way he'd secretly dreamed of for the past five years. Longer than that— since the first time he'd set eyes on her during freshman year at Stanford.

"Justin." She drew back just enough to look into his eyes. "I'm so glad you're here." Then she pulled him close and rested her cheek on his chest. "Promise me we won't ever go that long again without seeing each other, without talking to each other."

"I promise."

He'd been an idiot to go dark on her in Germany. Just as he'd been a fool to assume that things would be awkward between them now, that their conversations would be stilted, that there would be lingering guilt or blame.

He should have known that Taylor would only ever welcome him with open arms, no matter how badly he'd screwed up. She'd always been forgiving, ready to see the best in people.

When she stepped back, her cheeks were flushed, and he was pretty sure he'd never seen her look more beautiful than she did standing in the Napa Valley sunlight, surrounded by flowers. It struck him how right she looked. More right, he suddenly realized, than she'd ever looked on campus or inside a chemistry lab.

"So this place is yours now?"

She grinned as she turned to take in the Victorian building, painted a cheery yellow with purple trim. "It sure is." He could see how proud she was, and he wanted to tell her how proud he was of her too. He could only guess at the work she must have put in to make the B&B look so sparkly and welcoming. "I can't tell you how fun it is that you're my first guest." She cleared her throat and asked in an officious way, "May I help you with your bags, sir?"

He laughed, glad for the easy emotion. He hadn't laughed much these past years, not the way he used to whenever the two of them were together. "I'll grab my things from the car later. How about a quick tour before the rest of your guests show up?"

"Tonight it's just you and the Belmonts, a family of four, so hopefully we'll get some time to catch up. I'll show you around the house first, and then we can head out into the backyard."

He reached to grab her hand, a touch that was instantly electric, at least for him. There was so much he had to apologize for, but first he needed her to know, "I was sorry to hear about your grandfather."

Her face fell, and she gripped his hand tightly. "I really miss him. And I still can't believe he left his home to me."

"He knew how much you loved it."

"I really do. Even more now that I've had these past few months to make it mine."

He hadn't yet let go of her hand, couldn't quite bring himself to break contact. "Why didn't you tell me about him? And your new career?"

A guilty look crossed her face. "Last we talked, you were on the verge of a big breakthrough in the lab. I figured I'd tell you about everything when you came up for air. And with Drew and Ashley's wedding, I knew I'd at least see you there."

He ran a hand through his hair, feeling like a complete ass. She wasn't the one who should be looking guilty, he was. "I'm sorry I've been such a bad friend." All because their one drunken kiss hadn't turned into the happy-ever-after he'd been hoping for. "I have no excuse for the way I've behaved since leaving the country. I should have made more of an effort."

"Stop it." She might look like a ray of sunshine, but she could be surprisingly firm. "I won't let you beat yourself up for doing such important work. You're on the verge of curing breast cancer. That's more important than helping me figure out the best paint color for my B&B."

He wasn't surprised that she didn't want to hear his apologies. She'd never been one to hold a grudge—if she had, maybe she would have dumped Boring Bruce one of the many times he'd disappointed her. Justin hated knowing that he was no better than her boyfriend.

Which was why he made himself say, "Much as I wish I was actually curing cancer, I'm not quite there yet. My research is just one piece of the puzzle."

"A really big, important piece."

"What you're doing is important too, Taylor. Your grandfather's legacy is living on because of you. And," he added with a grin, "the purple paint looks great with the yellow."

"Thank you." She beamed at him as if he'd just given her the greatest compliment ever. "I just made chocolate chip cookies, if you're hungry after your drive."

His mouth was already watering as he asked, "Double chunk?"

"I wouldn't make them any other way."

How he didn't kiss her then, he had no idea.

Somehow, he kept his mouth off hers as they headed up the porch steps and she pointed out the fountain she'd installed in the garden, along with new floorboards on the porch and new sashes in all of the windows.

"You did all of this by yourself?" He'd always loved working with his hands—his father had passed on his love of woodworking to Justin when he was just a little kid. This would have been a heck of a great project.

"I never knew I had any of it in me until I got here," she said as they walked into the bright and welcoming entry. "Never even held a hammer before. At first, I was really intimidated by each new thing I needed to learn, but along the way, I realized that as long as I don't give up, I can do almost anything I set my mind to."

"Of course you can." He'd known that about her all along. The only thing he was surprised by was that she hadn't known it too, until she'd decided to open the B&B.

She gave him another radiant smile, then picked up a tray of cookies sitting on a table by the front window and held it out to him. The sound that came out of his mouth as he bit into one would have been embarrassing if he'd made it in front of anyone but Taylor. *"Thisissoogood."* He shoved the rest of the cookie into his mouth while he was still talking, already reaching for another.

She laughed, looking delighted as she watched him gorge on the cookies. "Do you have any idea how much I've missed you? If you're not careful, I might not let you get back on that plane to Germany next week."

His chest ached at the thought of leaving her. His vow not to fall head over heels in love with her again hadn't lasted even ten minutes.

"I won't be on the other side of the world forever."

"I know you won't. It just feels like it sometimes." Her phone buzzed in her pocket, and after she looked at the message, she said, "My other guests will be here in fifteen minutes, so let's do a quick tour, and then I'll come find you once I've got them settled in. Come into the kitchen, and I'll show you what I've done to it."

She gestured to the tiled countertops, white cupboards, and old-fashioned red oven. "I was able to salvage the cupboards by sanding and repainting them. Most of the tiles were in pretty good shape, thankfully, and I replaced the ones that were too badly cracked with special accent tiles. And the Heartland dual-fuel range is a classic that I would have never gotten rid of in a million years." She ran her hand over its glossy surface. "It took a while to stop burning everything, but now that I've got her figured out, I can't imagine going back to cooking with a modern stainless-steel oven."

"Apart from making the best double chocolate chunk cookies in the world, I didn't know you could cook."

"I couldn't. But evidently, bed-and-breakfast guests expect a well-cooked meal in the morning," she said with a crooked grin. "Fortunately, the Culinary Institute of America is just up the block. I've taken so many classes there in the past few months, I'm on a first-name basis with the entire staff. Like I said, tenacity is my middle name lately." She led him from the kitchen into a dining room, set up with several small, square tables that could be combined into larger ones if necessary. "Here's the breakfast room. It's also where I'm planning on doing afternoon tea for more than just guests a couple of times a week once I've got the rest of this B&B gig down." The windows looked out on the back garden—complete with a swimming pool. "We came in through the parlor." She grinned at him as she added, "Just like today, that's where the cookies will be every afternoon, along with coffee and tea."

"Good to know." He grabbed another cookie as they headed outside into a riot of color. "Your grandfather must have been a heck of a gardener."

"He was certainly ambitious. Even after cutting everything back a ton, I ended up having to pull out about half of it. I've been poring over gardening books at night, but when it comes to the outdoors, I'm just faking it until I make it. Turns out I'm way better with a hammer than a trowel."

"You're a woman of many hidden talents, aren't you?"

"More like a desperate woman." She picked a lavender stem and held it up to her nose. "I wasn't happy in Silicon Valley anymore, but I didn't want to go back to Rochester either," she admitted in a soft voice. "So when Grandpa left me this house, I pretty much decided I would do whatever it took to make it work."

"What about Bruce?" Despite the fact that Justin wasn't going to be an idiot again and make another play for her, he still needed to know where things stood between Taylor and her boyfriend. Namely, how close were they to the altar? Even the thought of it made his gut twist. "Is he still in Rochester, or has he moved out here?"

"This B&B was the final nail in our coffin. One I should have pounded in a long time ago."

Justin could barely keep from pumping his fist into the air. Which wasn't at all the appropriate response when coming here, seeing her again, was supposed to be about rekindling their friendship—and nothing more. Likewise, he shouldn't ask the question that was burning a hole in his tongue. "Any winemakers swept you off your feet?"

"Dating is the last thing I've been worried about. Between getting this place redone and dealing with—" She abruptly cut herself off, coloring slightly before saying, "What about you? Any pretty fräuleins getting lucky with you in Germany?"

Was it just his imagination, or did her voice suddenly sound a little funny? As though she was invested in his answer in a way that went beyond friendship.

"I haven't had much time to date."

"Come on, this is me you're talking to." She shot him a knowing look. "You had to beat girls off with a stick in college. I can't imagine things would be any different now. Surely you haven't been a monk for the past five years."

Of course he hadn't, but none of the women he'd been with had meant anything serious to him. He hadn't led them on, so there weren't any broken hearts as far as he knew. He'd told himself he was too busy with work to worry about a relationship, had convinced himself that he had gotten over, gotten past, his unrequited feelings for Taylor. But now that he was with her again, he had to admit the truth to himself.

He had been waiting for her.

And despite knowing better, he always would.

* * *

Why was she going on and on about Justin's prowess with women?

The problem was that he looked so good, Taylor was afraid that if she didn't keep saying all those other inane things, she might accidentally blurt, *I love you. I've always loved you!*

She felt her cheeks burn with mortification at the mere thought of it. She could only imagine how awkward things would get if she ever lost hold of herself and admitted how deep her feelings for him ran. There were few things Taylor regretted more than having forced that kiss on him during their last night together in Palo Alto, especially when she'd seen countless girls try any- and everything they could to snare him.

"Hey." He reached out to brush a lock of hair away from her face. "You okay?"

If he only knew just how not-okay she was. But she didn't want to ruin their reunion with bad news and tears. "I am." And when she looked into his eyes, she realized it was true. Because despite the constant worries that had been hanging over her since her diagnosis, and the huge amount of self-control she needed to exert not to throw herself into his arms, just being close to Justin again made her happier than she'd been in years. "Why don't I show you to your room so that you can settle in?"

He stared at her for a long moment, as though he knew she was keeping something from him, before dropping his hand from her cheek. "Is there any way I could help? Maybe by bringing up your other guests' bags?"

"Thanks, but based on what I know about your nonstop work schedule, you should take some time to relax while you can. There are some great wine-tasting rooms down the street, or restaurants I could recommend if you're hungry."

"I'm happy to stay right here in your garden, eating cookies."

Hugely grateful that the weird place they'd left each other in five years ago seemed to be nothing but water under the bridge, she looped her arm through his the way she used to, took him back inside and up the stairs. His room on the second floor overlooked the garden and pool. "The furniture is all antique, but the mattress is brand new. The Belmonts will be staying in two connected rooms on the other side of the landing, so it should be nice and quiet here for you."

"Where's your room?"

She pointed out the window. "I converted the old garage out back into a one-bedroom studio for myself." The bell over the front door chimed. "They're here! Wish me luck."

"Good luck, Taylor." He leaned forward and kissed her forehead. "I'm happy for you. You're going to do great here, I just know it."

"Thank you." It was barely a whisper. Her heart was so full from his lovely words…and the friendly kiss had her body far more revved up than it should be.

CHAPTER FOUR

Justin was impressed as he looked around his bedroom. Taylor clearly had a knack for creating spaces that were both comfortable and luxurious. If this were anyone else's B&B—and he was this jet-lagged—he'd be looking forward to getting a great night's sleep in the big, plush bed.

But he already knew he was going to spend the night tossing and turning as he thought about Taylor in her bed in the backyard cottage…wishing that she was in his.

Even though she'd turned down his offer to chip in, it was tempting to go downstairs to help her with her guests, simply because he didn't want to miss a minute of being near her this week. But he didn't want it to look like he thought she wasn't capable of running her business on her own, so he grabbed one of the paperback thrillers on a bookshelf in the hallway and headed down the stairs, intending to go out into the garden. He stopped at the base of the stairs when he heard her new guests gushing over the place.

"Your bed-and-breakfast is even prettier than the pictures online," the woman said.

"And it's such a great deal compared to the other places in town." A moment later, the man called out a slightly panicked, "Sophia, Addison, don't smear chocolate on the furniture!" He raced toward the kids with one of the napkins Taylor had put out next to the tray of cookies. "The kids are five and three, but we won't let them make a mess of your place," he promised her.

"Don't worry," Taylor said in her easygoing way. "I wouldn't have made chocolate chunk cookies for you if I was worried about stains."

"You made this?" A little girl with big brown eyes and chocolate across her cheek looked awestruck. "It's the most super yummy cookie *ever!*"

Taylor laughed, clearly delighted with the five-year-old's praise. "Thank you, Sophia. You're very sweet." She turned to her brother, who had a mischievous glint in his eyes. "Do you like Lego, Addison?" When he nodded so fast it looked like his head might wobble off his neck, she pointed at a big red plastic container in the corner of the parlor. "I've got lots of blocks right over there for you to play with."

Taylor handed the adults glasses of champagne. "Why don't the two of you relax for a few minutes while I take your luggage upstairs?" The couple looked beyond grateful for the chance to sit quietly and sip glasses of bubbly while their kids played happily in a sunny corner of the room.

Justin knew he shouldn't still be standing by the stairs watching them, but he couldn't move. Not when he'd just been hit with a vision, one so clear it staggered him—of himself and Taylor married with two kids of their own, on a family getaway.

He not only saw it, he *wanted* it. Wanted it with everything in him.

No question about it, his sisters had been right to send him to St. Helena for the week. He'd been defensive last night when they'd told him he needed to remember that there was more to life than the four walls of a lab. He'd told himself that his work was everything, that saving other people's lives was more important than living his own. But though his research *was* important, and he would never turn his back on it, coming here and seeing Taylor again made him remember that he used to be a man who craved more than just work.

He needed affection. Laughter.

And most of all, love, no matter how impossible that might seem at the moment.

"Justin?" Taylor was standing in front of him now, her head cocked as she asked, "Is there something you need?"

Yes. I need you to be mine. To have and to hold and to love, and then to carry that love forward with our kids, and then our grandkids after that.

When he looked at Taylor, he suddenly saw more than he had even five minutes ago. She was still the beautiful, sweet, brilliant woman he was desperately attracted to...but what he now wanted went far beyond just sharing her bed.

The words were there, right on the tip of his tongue, and he barely managed to hold them back. He didn't want to freak her out, not when they'd only just begun to reconnect. That night at the bar back in college, he'd been too desperate, had moved too fast. This week, he'd force himself to take his time to find a way, any way he could, to bring her around to the idea of them. *Together.* As more than just friends.

"Just heading into the garden with a book." He was pleased his voice sounded so easy. Not at all like a guy madly plotting to get the woman of his dreams to fall in love with him.

She craned her neck to see the title. "Oh, that's a good one. Scary enough that I kept catching myself holding my breath while I was reading it. I hope you don't mind losing some sleep."

"I'm used to making do without much sleep," he said with a shrug. Catching up on sleep this week was already a lost cause with her so close, but still untouchable. At least, until he reminded her just how good they were together—and proved to her that making the jump from friends to lovers, and then so much more, was the right thing for both of them.

"I'll come out and join you when I get a chance." Smiling, she picked up the two large suitcases and started up the stairs.

Every ounce of chivalry inside of him bucked at watching her carry the bags without his help. He had just about lost the fight when she let out an agonizing sound of pain and dropped them both.

Justin caught the suitcases before they could tumble down the stairs. Taylor was clutching her side and gasping as she sat on the nearest step. "What happened?" He knelt in front of her. "Tell me how I can help. Tell me what you need."

"I'm—" Even talking seemed to hurt, and his chest clenched tight at seeing her in such pain. "I'm okay. It's hot out, and I haven't had enough to drink today. Can you please get me a glass of water?"

He hated leaving her sitting there alone, but he'd just told her he'd do anything she asked. "I'll be right back."

He'd never moved so fast in his life as he did to get that glass of water. She gave him a grateful but trembling smile as she took it and slowly drank. Thankfully, the color soon came back into her cheeks.

"Now that I've had more time to think about it," she said a few moments later, "how about you help me with the suitcases?"

"Anything you need, I'm here for you." His words were utterly serious, full of the emotional weight he'd previously been warning himself not to heap on her. But all he could see inside his head was a loop of her crying out and collapsing on the stairs. "You know that, don't you?"

"Of course I do." She reached for his hand. "Same goes for me with you."

He couldn't look away from her eyes, didn't ever want to let go of her hand. Until a wail sounded from the front parlor.

"I should probably show the Belmont family to their room and then get them off to a restaurant before their kids really start to riot."

Justin reluctantly let her go and picked up the bags. "Their luggage will be waiting upstairs." But he couldn't let her leave until he said, "Promise me you'll come find me right away if you feel any more pain."

"I will."

★ ★ ★

Taylor couldn't get Justin's worried expression out of her head.

She was taking a few quiet minutes to herself in the kitchen after seeing the Belmonts off to a burger place on Main Street. Looking out the window, she could see Justin sitting by the fountain, the paperback open on his lap. From her secret viewing spot, she had a chance to appreciate his good looks. Or at least she would have if she could stop rewinding to his horror when the pain had her dropping the suitcases and collapsing on the stairs.

She'd had a good run this past week with no sharp pains and had hoped that with all her care, the deterioration of her kidney function might be slowing. But with her next checkup in a couple of days, she was dreading finding out her new markers. If they kept falling so fast…

No. She couldn't let herself think like that. Couldn't fall into a pit of self-pity.

She couldn't face telling Justin yet either. Not tonight. Not when he'd looked so worried on the stairs. And not when he'd been the one to find his mother on the kitchen floor, passed out from the internal ravages of a cancer none of them had known was there.

Was it too much to ask for a few hours, maybe even a few days of fun with her best friend? Because as soon as she told him about her diagnosis, she knew what he'd do—the same thing he'd done for his mother. He'd spend twenty-four seven looking for cures, for medicines and diet plans and anything else that had even a ghost of a chance of making the disease go away. When what he really needed to do was take the chance to truly unwind and relax for the first time in years.

Standing at the sink, Taylor did a quick scan of her body. Thankfully, she felt steady again. Steady enough, certainly, to have a nice catch-up with her bestie.

Grabbing the rest of the bottle of bubbly and two glasses, she headed into the garden. "How does champagne in the garden and pizza delivery for dinner sound?"

He put down the book. "Are your guests off exploring town?"

"They are. So it'll be just you and me for the next couple of hours."

"Just you and me sounds perfect."

If she didn't know better, she'd think he *meant* to give her that sexy smile. But she knew she was only imagining what she wanted to see, because when she looked closer, he was looking at her in exactly the same friendly way he always had.

She poured champagne, but when she went to hand him his, she was surprised to see a small velvet pouch in his hand. "Something special to celebrate your new home and business."

There was no reason for her to feel nervous about

Justin giving her a small gift. After all, they'd often surprised each other with a box of favorite chocolates or a book they thought the other person might enjoy. Still, her hand wasn't exactly steady as she reached for it. "You didn't need to bring me anything," she said as she sat across from him at the bright yellow café table.

"I've wanted you to have it for a long time."

Gently tugging on the ribbons, the last thing she expected to see when the pouch fell open was a ring. A vibrant orange and red fire opal in the most perfect, delicate platinum setting.

"This was your mother's." She looked up at Justin, stunned that he could even think of giving it to her. She held out her hands, the ring still carefully contained in the velvet. "I can't take this from you. You need to keep it." It was *far* more than just a housewarming gift.

But he didn't take it back. Instead, he said, "She knew she didn't have long when she gave it to me. She said that one day she hoped it would be a perfect fit for someone I really cared about. We both knew who she meant. You."

"How can you be so sure?"

He smiled. "Do you remember junior year, when you finally confessed to having a rock collection?"

She thought back to that day when he'd gotten her to confess to just how much of a geek she really was.

"So embarrassing."

"Not nearly as embarrassing as my *Star Trek* figurine collection."

"True," she agreed with a laugh.

"I asked you what your favorite stone was, but somehow, I already knew. Even before you told me."

"Fire opal." It had been his mother's favorite stone too.

"I wanted to give you the ring that day, but…" He looked down at the opal, which Taylor could have sworn was glowing in the early evening light, almost as though it were alive. As though Lisa Morrison were sitting out in the garden with them. "I was still reeling. I couldn't even talk about Mom back then without losing it."

"You could always talk to me, Justin." Taylor took one of his hands in hers. "Then and now."

"I know." He looked up into her eyes. "That's why I want you to have her ring. That's why *she* wanted you to have it too."

Her heart was beating so fast you would have thought he was proposing. "I'd be honored to wear your mother's ring." Her eyes were damp as he reached for her right hand and slid the ring onto her third finger.

"She was right," he said in a deep voice that resonated with emotion. "It fits you perfectly."

CHAPTER FIVE

Justin had intended to keep things light and fun to start. But he hadn't been able to stop himself from baring a piece of his heart to Taylor.

By the time she came outside, the sun had gone down, and he'd been sitting out in the garden for an hour rereading the same page. He'd read other books by this author and knew it was probably a gripping story. But all he could see when he looked at the page was Taylor in pain. And though it had been nothing more serious than cramps from dehydration, the sight of her hurting bothered him. A lot.

Thankfully, she seemed to be herself again, with bright eyes and a big smile. She kept looking down at the ring on her hand as it sparkled in the light of the moon and the lights she'd strung throughout the garden, almost as if she couldn't believe it was real. He felt his heart swell knowing how much she loved it.

His mother would have absolutely loved to see Taylor wearing her ring. At long last.

"So," he said, deliberately pivoting away from big emotional moments for the time being, "how are your folks doing? And your brother?"

"They're good." She took a small sip of champagne, then set the glass down. "My dad is getting close to retirement and pretty much lives at the golf course already. My mom was thinking of running for city council, but decided to put that off."

"Why?" He'd met Caroline Cardenes several times. It had been obvious that Taylor's mother hadn't approved of him or his friendship with her daughter—she'd seemed to think that he was a playboy who was angling to lead Taylor into the path of danger. He'd tried to make her understand that keeping Taylor safe and well was as much his priority as it was hers, but she'd never warmed to him, always polite but brittle whenever they spoke.

Taylor picked up her glass and took another tiny sip before answering. "The city council would be a big-time commitment, and I think she wants to wait until her decks are cleared a bit more."

"Is something going on with your brother?" Austin was five years younger than Taylor and had always been a bit of a troublemaker. Possibly, Justin thought, because her parents had always been overprotective of their kids. It was only here in St. Helena in her new B&B that Taylor seemed to have pushed her way free of her parents' protective borders.

"Actually, Austin is doing really well. College wasn't a great fit for him, but now that he's started working at a gaming company, he seems to have found his niche." She refilled his glass. "What about you? I need the full rundown on all of your brothers and sisters. I talked briefly with Olivia and Maddie when they called to check in about your week here, but we weren't able to catch up properly. Start with Maddie. She sounded so mature on the phone."

"You're going to freak when you see her at Drew and Ashley's wedding," he said. "One second she was a little girl and the next she wasn't."

"How are you dealing with that, Mr. Protective Big Brother?"

"Badly." They both laughed, though he was speaking the truth. "No one will ever be good enough for her, but telling her that would be as good as shoving her into some loser's arms."

"You're right. There's nothing you can do but suck it up when she brings home Mr. Wrong." She shook her head and made a face. "It's something every girl's got to learn for herself."

"What happened with your ex?" Now that she'd given him that Mr. Wrong lead-in, he had to know. "Why did you break up?"

She looked over at the pool, almost as if she didn't

want to look him in the eye when she answered. "After graduation, Bruce had all these plans for us in Rochester. Really detailed ones where I swear he must have sat down with my parents to map it all out—where we were going to live, work, how many kids we were going to have." She grimaced. "Everyone heard wedding bells."

He wanted to be angry at Bruce, at her parents, on Taylor's behalf. But how could he blame them when he was sitting here wanting the exact same thing, wanting those wedding bells ringing for him and her?

"I was the only one who didn't hear them," she continued. As if she could read Justin's mind, she said, "I know you didn't like him. But he's a nice guy, has a good heart, means well. And staying with him was safe, the kind of safety that I knew my parents wanted for me. Being with Bruce kept me tethered to Rochester, and it gave them hope that I wouldn't leave forever." She sighed. "You know it isn't really about me. They're still just so destroyed from losing the baby they had before I was born." Justin was one of the very few people who knew this about her family. "I think part of the reason I've played it safe is because I hate the thought of causing my parents another moment of grief. Even though we've never actually sat down and talked about their lost child, it feels like it's colored everything in our lives."

"I know what it's like not to want to talk about the hard stuff," he said. All too well, considering he and his father still hadn't ever really talked about their grief. "My mom was always after us to speak up, though, even if we were scared. *Especially* if we were scared." It was only after her death that they'd all clammed up on each other. Sean and Drew had been lucky to have Serena and Ashley to help them deal with their grief. Justin had been lucky too—without Taylor by his side, he didn't know how he would have coped that first year.

But that wasn't the only thing Justin had been afraid to talk about—he and Taylor had never brought up their kiss. Not once since it happened. And he couldn't help but think that had been a mistake. A huge one. Because what if they'd both gotten it wrong? What if they'd wasted the past five years because neither of them had been brave enough to have a potentially difficult conversation?

He wouldn't bring it up tonight, not when he really did want to give Taylor some time to see how good they were together first. But he wouldn't wait much longer. He'd already waited so many years...

"So many times in the past few months," she said, breaking into his thoughts, "I've thought about trying to talk with my mom about the sister I never knew, but something always stops me."

Again, he nodded. "It's tough. I mean, my dad and I still haven't ever really talked about losing my mom. So I completely get where you are with it." But he hadn't gotten the full story about her ex yet, so he said, "Even though you thought it would worry your parents, you still broke up with Bruce."

She rubbed her neck, looking uncomfortable. "This is going to sound really lame after everything you and your family have been through, but the truth is that breaking up with Bruce was the scariest thing I'd ever done, because it meant I finally had to figure out how to live my own life on my own terms."

"You already knew how to do that," Justin argued.

"Not really. College was just another map some-one else drew for me—take this class, graduate with this major, apply for this job. I thought I was being bold by staying in Palo Alto after graduation instead of moving back to Rochester, but even after I got the job in the lab and was living in College Terrace, it just didn't fit properly. None of it did until I came here." She dropped her hand from her neck, as though at last she'd reached the part of the story where she could relax. "Don't get me wrong, I'm totally flailing. Still trying like crazy to figure everything out long after I already should have. And probably screwing up more than I'm getting right. But I'm having fun. More fun than I've had since you left for Germany."

His eyebrows rose. That was quite an admission—that he'd been the most fun part of her life, until now, at least. "I haven't had much fun since then either. But today is a pretty great move in the right direction."

They smiled at each other, a moment filled with enduring friendship. But also, he could have sworn, something more. Something deeper, richer, *sexier*. Something Justin hoped Taylor wouldn't want to deny any more than he did.

The front bell chimed, and with the windows open, they could hear it in the garden. "That must be the pizza," she said. "I'll be right back."

"You've been running around all day. I'll get this." He left before she could argue and came back a few minutes later with the huge pizza box. "I figured we'd eat straight out of the box the way we always used to. No point in getting plates dirty."

Nodding, she flipped open the cover and grabbed a piece. Hot cheese dripped and fell onto the cardboard as she took a bite. "*Mmmm. So good.*"

He had been about to grab his own piece, but the pleasure-filled sound she'd just made shifted his focus to an entirely different kind of hunger.

When she noticed he wasn't eating, she said, "Aren't you hungry?"

"Starved." So starved for *her* that he couldn't even think of reaching for pizza.

Her eyes locked with his again, and then she was suddenly shoving her chair back, her expression distinctly uncomfortable. "This pizza is making me really thirsty. I'd better get us some water, otherwise we're going to be chugging champagne. And we all know what a lightweight I am!"

Her laughter sounded slightly forced, and then she was hurrying off, obviously intent on putting some space between them for a few minutes.

Justin let out a low curse in the middle of the garden. So much for playing it cool and taking time to convince her they were perfect together. All he'd managed so far was to make her feel so uncomfortable that she ran away.

When she came back with the ice water, rather than drinking it, he would be better off dumping it over his head.

* * *

Taylor knew she couldn't keep hiding in the kitchen whenever her feelings for Justin got too big, too hot, too intense. All he'd said was that he was *starved* and she'd practically gone up in flames. Even though she very much doubted there had been any undertones or hidden meanings.

When Justin had asked her why she and her boyfriend had finally broken up, all of the reasons she'd given him were true, but she'd deliberately left out the biggest one: *He wasn't you.*

Back in college, she'd been too big a coward to let Justin know how she felt. Holding on to her boyfriend had meant that Justin would never consider her anything more than a friend—which also meant that he would never crush her heart if she confessed her feelings and he didn't return them.

Now, for the first time since their friendship began, they were both single. Four months ago, she might have decided this was her big chance to declare her feelings, and risk having her heart destroyed when he didn't return them.

But that was before her diagnosis. PKD could be so debilitating—according to her doctor, she'd been losing kidney function at warp speed these past few months— that unless she had a successful transplant, and soon, any crush she had on Justin, especially if he magically felt the same way, could be moot. He'd already lost his mother to a devastating disease. She couldn't let him risk loving another woman whose body was a ticking time bomb.

Reminding herself of all the reasons that being with Justin as more than a friend would never come to fruition helped settle her down as she filled a pitcher with ice water and grabbed two more glasses. This week was all about rekindling a precious friendship, nothing more. She wouldn't let herself get all hot and bothered again.

Feeling better, she went outside. "We were talking about Maddie when the conversation somehow steered off course. She told me a little bit about her restaurant work, and it sounds amazing."

"I'm really proud of her," he said with a grin. It was one of the things she loved most about him—how close he was to his siblings. "She's been working at a restaurant in the city, but I know she's also been trying her hand at baking on commission for some stores and businesses in the area."

"Everything she used to make when she was in high school was so good, I can't wait to see—that should be *taste*, actually—where she's taken her talent by now." Her slice of pizza was cold as she picked it up, but keeping reminders of heat to a minimum was for the best. "Tell me about Sean next. Although, since I've been seeing his photographs everywhere, I have a pretty good idea how he's doing, at least professionally."

"He's on fire." Justin took another slice out of the box. "We always knew he was talented, but it's nice that the rest of the world agrees. Seeing his work on the cover of *National Geographic* was epic. He tried to play it cool when he called to tell me, but then Serena grabbed the phone and couldn't stop bubbling over about it."

"They really are the perfect couple, aren't they?"

"Always were," he agreed, "even though their start was messy."

Taylor knew all about how Sean and Serena had gotten together at a Stanford frat party when Serena was a freshman and Sean was a junior. Serena had been the world's most innocent supermodel-turned-coed, and Sean had been drunk and reeling from his mother's death. The next morning, when he'd gone to apologize for coming on too strong and found an overzealous fan bothering her, he'd instinctively protected her—and they'd ended up forging a friendship. One that had quickly and beautifully turned into love.

"I read Serena's book. It was fantastic!" Taylor had always been a fan of historical fiction, and even though she was biased, she believed Serena had written a truly compelling Victorian-set mystery. "It almost felt as though she'd lived in Victorian England."

"They spent a lot of time in England a couple of years back, Serena doing research while Sean took pictures."

"It's all so romantic," Taylor said with a sigh. One she hoped didn't sound too envious. "Now give me the dirt on Olivia. I know she's still working on her PhD, but even though I couldn't squeeze too much out of her over the phone, I couldn't help but think she's focused on more than just work right now."

He raised an eyebrow. "I think there might be a secret guy stashed in the shadows somewhere."

"She told you that?" Olivia and Madison knew firsthand how nuts their brothers could be about vetting the guys they dated. Taylor had always figured Olivia wouldn't let on that she was serious about someone until it was a *fait accompli*, maybe even after eloping, just so her four brothers wouldn't try to change her mind.

"No," he admitted. "But she was even cagier than usual."

"I'll have to see what I can get out of her at the wedding." Before he could say anything, she added, "And don't even think of asking about what I find out, because I'm sure she'll make me promise not to tell you a thing."

"You've never been able to keep a secret from me," he said in that low drawl that always gave her thrill bumps.

Somehow, she managed to keep the smile on her face. Thank God he'd never guessed the biggest secret of all: just how much deeper her feelings for him went than *friend*. She'd better move on or risk falling into dangerous territory. "I already know Drew and Ashley are blissfully happy, and I'd have to be deaf not to hear his songs everywhere."

"It's the same in Germany—in every cafe, restaurant, store, even at work in the lab—his songs are playing. I used to brag about being his brother, but I finally realized I should stop."

"Why?"

"No one ever believes me once they hear me sing."

"Sing something for me now."

"I can't believe I forgot how evil you can be," he teased.

"Please. No one has ever covered Celine Dion quite like you."

Before she could prepare herself, he launched into "My Heart Will Go On," making her gasp at just how horrible it sounded even as she laughed herself silly. On nights when she'd wound herself up tight with lab work and test prep at Stanford, he would often surprise her with a Celine Dion song. Hearing him butcher "The Power of Love" or "It's All Coming Back to Me Now" never failed to loosen her up.

It wasn't until a couple of dogs in the neighborhood howled that she realized she should shush him. By then, however, he was up out of his seat, putting on theatrical Las Vegas-style moves to go with the words.

Her stomach hurt from laughing so hard. "God, I've missed you," she said, wrapping her arms around herself.

"Is your side hurting again?" He'd gone from

laughter to concern in a second.

"No." She was glad it was the truth for once—and also that there was still one more Morrison to ask about to deflect Justin's attention from her. "I'm assuming Grant is continuing to take over the business world?"

"You know Grant. He's always on the lookout for another business model to blow up, another industry to turn inside out, another research endeavor to fund."

"But do you think he's happy?" Grant had never been anything but kind to her. At the same time, she could never quite read him.

Justin paused to think about her question. "I know it's important to him that he makes good changes in the world. But I suppose it doesn't leave much time for anything else."

"Life's too short to waste any of it," she said softly.

"I agree," Justin said. And then the next thing she knew, he was taking her hand and pulling her from her chair and into his arms.

Wanting nothing more than to melt into him, she made herself stay stiff. "What are you doing?"

"I want to dance with my best friend. And since we both agree that life is short…" He drew her close so that her cheek rested against his chest and she had no choice but to relax into giggles as he started humming Celine Dion again, brutally off-key.

"Why don't we let the frogs and crickets take care of the music?" she suggested.

And as they swayed together in the faint light of the moon, Taylor knew no night had ever been this perfect. At the end of the week, he would be gone, but she would cherish this moment in his arms forever.

CHAPTER SIX

Leaving Taylor with nothing more than a kiss on her forehead the previous evening had been one of the hardest things Justin had ever done.

He'd woken up grouchy, but as soon as he'd eaten the incredible breakfast she made, everything turned around. The omelet, bacon, and scones were so good he could swear she was the next coming of Julia Child.

The Belmont family, with whom he'd sat at breakfast, had perked him up too. The kids reminded him of the way he and his siblings had been when they were young. Rambunctious, but not meaning any harm. The little girl in particular captivated Justin.

Now, he was helping Taylor do dishes before they headed out for the day to see the wine country's sights. He was glad that she had found Rufus and Janet, a husband-and-wife cleaning team, to help out with the rooms every morning after her guests left to sightsee. He hated to think of her trying single-handedly to take care of everything, even though he knew she was more than capable of it.

Taylor grinned at him from her spot at the kitchen sink. "You had quite a little admirer at breakfast."

"It's mutual. Sophia's going to grow up to be a heartbreaker, that's for sure."

"Starting with yours when they leave, if your plans to help her set up a lemonade stand on the sidewalk tomorrow afternoon are anything to go by."

"What can I say—I'm a sucker for brown eyes and a big smile."

If Taylor had any idea that he wasn't just talking about the little girl now, but the beautiful woman standing beside him at the sink, she didn't give any indication. "What do you want to do first?" she asked after they'd dried and put away all of the breakfast dishes and frying pans. "See the petrified forest? Or the geyser? Or maybe even take a mud bath?"

He'd seen the pamphlets for the famous Calistoga mud baths, all of which showed couples enjoying them together. Hoping against hope that this was what she was hinting at, he said, "I'd be up for a mud bath if you are."

She shuddered. "No way am I getting into a vat of dirt." She shot him a teasing look. "But I'd be happy to dunk you in one."

"Are you still trying to get back at me for *accidentally* losing your clothes at the beach that day?" He hadn't deliberately dropped her clothes into a crevasse between boulders—the wind had blown her shorts and T-shirt out of his hands before he could stop it. Though she'd had on a bikini, she'd still been mortified about making the long walk back to the car in just her bathing suit. All he'd had to give her for the drive home was his T-shirt. He'd be lying if he said he hadn't appreciated stealing glances at her completely bare legs next to him all the way home.

She made a mock-angry face, one that was so cute he almost lost the fight against leaning over and kissing her. "Trust me," she said, "the day I get you back for that will be far worse than just dumping mud all over you. I've had years to plan…"

When he'd been in his lab in Germany, hunched over his computer and microscope, he'd almost forgotten how good it was to be with her, even if all they were doing was washing dishes and joking with each other. Hell, just holding her in his arms last night while they were dancing had been miles better than anything he'd ever experienced in bed with another woman.

"How about we start with the geyser?" she suggested. "And then we can grab some sandwiches on the way to the petrified forest. We should have plenty of time to see both before I have to head back to get things ready for afternoon tea."

The hours flew by, full of laughter and inside jokes Justin had only with her. He'd barely seen the sunlight during the years he'd been holed up in the lab, but even if he'd been traveling the world nonstop, the beauty of Napa Valley would have floored him. Hills covered in pine, redwood, and oak trees rose up from sweeping plains covered in grapevines. Artisan cheese and chocolate and olive oil shops were everywhere, along with some of the best restaurants in the world. Everywhere he looked, something was in bloom, from vegetable gardens to front-yard flower gardens.

And Taylor had never looked so perfectly in her element.

Justin had thought she was happy at Stanford. She was so intelligent that biology had seemed like a good fit. But after watching her interact with her guests this morning over breakfast, and then with the locals in their stores as she bought fresh honey and cheese and sausage, he realized he hadn't known her nearly as well as he'd thought.

Almost as though there was a part of herself that she'd always kept hidden from him. Just as he'd always kept a part of himself from her, out of fear that the depth of his desire, his emotions, would drive her away instead of bringing her closer.

He couldn't wait much longer to tell her how he felt. After a long sunny morning and afternoon where they didn't just reminisce about old memories, but started making new ones, he felt good. Better than he'd felt in years. Tonight, when the right moment came to confess his feelings, he would take it.

* * *

It had been a perfect day. Taylor's first breakfast for her guests had gone smoothly, both inside of the kitchen and out. She'd booked a group of women from San Francisco who were coming to Napa for a girls' weekend later in the month. And, best of all, she'd had a wonderful time touring the valley with Justin.

Taylor wanted to get one hundred percent well for herself, of course, and for her mother, father, and brother, who were all praying that she'd find a match who would be willing to undergo the kidney-donation procedure. But Justin was one of the biggest reasons of all. She wanted to be his friend not only for the next five years, but for the next fifty as well.

He'd helped her set out and serve afternoon tea and coffee and cookies for the Belmonts, who had just headed into town for an early dinner. Now the two of them were working together in her garden, Taylor pulling weeds while Justin deadheaded the copious rose bushes.

"I'm always terrified I'm going to screw up the roses because I don't know what I'm doing. And I always prick myself, which is why I've left them so long," she said as she watched him move efficiently from one bush to the next. "If I'd known you were this good a gardener, I would have sent you a plane ticket four months ago."

"Come here, and I'll show you a few tricks."

It was perfectly natural to walk into the open curve of his arms so that her back was nearly pressed to his front. Unfortunately, it was also unavoidable that every square inch of her body would heat up from his close proximity. If only he didn't smell so good, and have such strong, tanned arms, and be standing so close that his breath whispering over her as he spoke sent heat coursing through her, head to toe.

"First of all, you really can't hurt a rose bush by overtrimming it." He sounded so relaxed, while her heart was beating a million miles a minute. In fact, her heartbeat was whooshing so loudly inside her own head that she wondered how he couldn't hear it. "Second, you need to make sure you've got on thick gloves." He took the gloves she'd forgotten to put on from her gardening bucket and slid them onto her hands. Just that tiny little bit of skin touching skin, she was stunned to realize, was better than any actual sex she'd ever had. "Third, you need to make sure you're using good, sharp hand pruners." He gave them to her. "Now, all that's left is finding a healthy bud and then making your cut a quarter of an inch above it."

With his nearness searing her, she lost whatever grace she might have possessed and jerked her bare forearm toward the prickly bush. Thankfully, Justin's reflexes were so fast that he was able to pull her back before any thorns pricked her.

"Try again." His voice moved through her like a well-aged port—smooth and warm, with an undeniable pull at her senses. "And this time, relax. I won't let anything happen to you."

She'd always known how lucky she was to have Justin in her life. During their years at Stanford, he had been the most steadfast of friends. It wasn't his fault that they'd fallen so out of touch with each other. She'd thought it was better that way, that some distance would help diffuse her unrequited feelings for him.

She knew better now. Distance had only made her heart grow fonder—not to mention ratcheting up her desire for him to near-desperate levels.

But she'd done so well all day, hadn't she? There hadn't been any long pauses where she'd let slip her inappropriate feelings, and she hadn't had to run away and hide to collect herself either. She'd simply let herself have fun and enjoy being with him, despite the fact that everything he did made her melt inside.

Forcing herself to relax against him, she was pleasantly surprised to see how easy it was to safely trim back her rose bushes when she followed his advice.

"See, what did I tell you?" he said once they were done and had both pulled off their gloves. "Nothing to it."

"Thank you for showing me." She turned her head to look up into his eyes as she spoke, and suddenly there it was—one of those long pauses she'd so triumphantly avoided. One that would be steeped in the deep emotion she'd been trying to hide from him. She spun out of his arms so fast she nearly toppled over.

"Taylor?"

She swatted at an invisible bug. "There was a bee." Fumbling to cover her lame lie, she quickly asked, "Where did you learn how to prune roses?"

"My mom. I used to help her out in the garden. None of the others had any interest, but I was always amazed by how things grew. I was a bio geek from the start." He was smiling as he said it, but she could see the pain that was always in his eyes when he talked about his mom.

"Sometimes," Taylor said softly, "I still can't believe she's gone."

All last night and today, she hadn't been able to keep from looking down at the beautiful ring on her finger. Not because of the weight of it—somehow, that was strangely familiar, as if it really did belong on her hand. But because of what she wished she could say to Lisa Morrison.

Taylor wished she could let his mother know that though Justin and his siblings were still hurting from her loss, they were all doing much better now. And she wished she could make his mom a promise that she would do whatever it took to be there for Justin, to always be his friend.

Justin's mother had always been so easy to talk to, to laugh with. Though Taylor's family had been on the other side of the country, Lisa Morrison had made her feel she wasn't so alone, especially those first few months of freshman year when everything had been so new and different. Taylor had been an automatic invite to every family party, every birthday, even the hotly contested family tennis tournament.

After Lisa had been diagnosed, Taylor had not only accompanied Justin to his mother's hospital room many times, she'd also gone alone to visit with her. Sometimes, they had chatted, laughed. Other times, they simply sat quietly together, Lisa's hand in Taylor's, this very ring on his mother's finger.

"She'd like knowing we're here together in your garden," Justin said. "Especially since she always wanted me to be with you."

Taylor nearly dropped the clippers. "She said that?"

"Well, she always told me how much she loved

you. And how she felt like you were one of the family."

Love for his mother tangled with disappointment that Lisa hadn't literally said she wanted Justin and Taylor to be together. "That's a pretty big leap to make," she said in as light a voice as she could manage. "Especially when everyone knows we've never been anything more than friends."

"Haven't we?"

This time, the clippers did fall. Nearly taking out the toes of her right foot, in fact. "Are you thirsty? Or hungry?" She didn't wait for him to reply. "I'll go put something together in the kitchen for us."

But instead of letting her run from him the way she had the night before, he reached out and grabbed her hand. "I haven't forgotten," he said in a low voice. "Do you remember, Taylor? What happened that night before I left for Germany..."

Oh God. Of course she remembered. How could she possibly forget the night she'd made an utter, absolute fool of herself?

It had been early in senior year, the night before the lab in Frankfurt had unexpectedly whisked him off. She'd been having trouble with her Bioinformatics class all quarter. Her brain couldn't quite connect the dots, and Justin had saved her by tutoring her. Their sessions usually went down over beer and burgers, but it was still extra work he didn't need to take on.

Wanting his time to be worth it, she'd worked twice as hard.

She'd been dreading the midterm exam, but Justin had prepared her far beyond what the professor expected. Justin had been waiting for her outside the classroom. She'd been unable to control her reaction, had literally leaped into his arms. *"I aced it."* She didn't need to get her grade back to be sure of it. He'd spun her around, grinning, as she said, *"Let's celebrate."*

She'd never been great at holding her liquor. She wasn't much to look at on the dance floor either. But she'd been on such a high that she'd forgotten both of those things that night. She couldn't remember how many tequila shots she'd tossed back, only that dancing made her thirsty and every shot made her want to dance more.

All the times she and Justin had gone out together, just the two of them or in a group, she'd always been careful not to behave as though they were a couple. There were no slow dances, no inappropriate touches or glances. But that night, her inhibitions finally fell. Far enough that when the other couples on the dance floor drew close, she couldn't stop herself from doing the same with Justin.

He'd let her put her arms around him, let her drunkenly hold on and sway to the music. And then, the next thing she knew, her mouth was on his...and she was kissing him with all the passion she'd been holding back for three years.

She'd tried to tell herself she'd done it only because she was drunk, too far gone to have any self-control. But if that were actually true, then she wouldn't have been so erotically aware of his taste, or the breathtaking feel of his lips crushed to hers, or the sensual slick of his tongue.

She hadn't wanted to pull away, hadn't ever wanted to stop kissing him. But when another couple bumped into them on the dance floor, jolting them apart, she knew she couldn't get away with it twice. She hadn't even been able to look him in the eye. She'd let her words slur and pretended to be on the verge of passing out. He'd taken her home and tucked her in, then watched over her while she'd feigned sleep.

The next morning, he'd let her make lame excuses about drinking too much, until Grant had called with the news that Justin needed to get on the next plane to Frankfurt because they wanted to fund his research and start work immediately. Everything had moved so fast after that, as she helped him with packing and hasty good-byes. Fast enough that neither of them had brought up the kiss again.

Not until today.

She scrunched her eyes shut, as mortified five years later as she'd been the morning after. "I'd hoped you had forgotten," she whispered. "I never should have behaved that way. Never should have gotten drunk and forced myself on you."

"You didn't force yourself on me, Taylor. I'm the one who took advantage of you when you were drunk."

"You didn't!" Her eyes shot open in her shock that he could think such a thing. "You were a perfect gentleman, just like always."

"Not that night, I wasn't. And I'm still not. Because even though I've had five years to repent what I did, I still can't help wanting to do it again. Do you have any idea how many times I've replayed our kiss in my head? How much I want to kiss you again?"

Somewhere in the back of her mind, Taylor knew there was more than one rational reason why they shouldn't do this. But her desperate need for him didn't only push all of those reasons away, it also pushed her back into his arms...and her mouth against his.

CHAPTER SEVEN

Soft.

Sweet.

Perfect.

Justin had dreamed of kissing Taylor again at least a thousand times. But his dreams had nothing on the incredible reality of her mouth against his, her arms wound around his neck, her curves pressed along the front of his body. She radiated heat—and desire fierce enough to rival his own.

Their kiss years ago on the dance floor had been the best of his life. Tonight, by comparison, it seemed nothing more than a drunken fumble, a flash of pleasure that came so quickly he'd barely had time to enjoy it before it was ripped away.

This was what a kiss was meant to be. A slow, heady exploration. A taste of heaven. An endless gasp of pleasure. Anticipation of all that was yet to come.

He didn't know who closed the distance between them first, but it didn't matter. Only that the distance was finally gone.

He'd held Taylor enough times to know that she was his perfect fit, but a friendly arm around her shoulders was worlds away from pulling her so close that he could run his hands slowly down her back, then over the flare of her hips. And when she made a sound of surprised pleasure, one that made him feel as though he was the first man ever to touch her like this, instinct took over completely.

The instinct to possess—and to pleasure.

As he kissed her again, he let those dual instincts override anything else—any thoughts, any concerns, any hesitations—that might have tried to intrude. They hadn't talked through what they were doing, but they would. Later, when words mattered again.

Tonight, all that mattered was stoking the flames that had finally been allowed to burst into beautiful, sizzling life after all the years when deep emotion and desperate attraction had secretly burned between them.

Hand in hand, they headed toward her small cottage at the back of the property. Her other guests had made it clear during afternoon tea that they wouldn't need her assistance again until the following morning, so she was free for the rest of the night. But he didn't want to take her back to his room in the house and risk being disturbed—and he didn't want her to think she needed to be quiet either. He wanted to love her so well, so completely, that she went hoarse from calling out his name and begging him for more.

After only a few steps, they had to stop and kiss again. When he finally forced himself to pull away so that he could keep making progress toward her bed, she put her hand on the back of his head and drew his lips back down to hers.

Nothing could have pleased him more than knowing he wasn't the only one who couldn't get enough. He wouldn't allow himself to mourn all the wasted years they could have been loving each other. Instead, he would relish every single second he had with her from this moment forward, a future filled with hot sex *and* laughter, friendship *and* love.

When it might otherwise have taken him thirty seconds to cross the garden, constantly kissing the woman of his dreams multiplied the time by ten, at least.

Soft, sweet kisses quickly became raw and desperate. Justin didn't hold anything back in his kisses, just as he didn't plan to hold anything back in the stroke of his hands over her naked curves, or when he finally made love to her. Tonight, they would finally commit to each other on every level—as friends, as lovers, as partners in everything.

All these years, he'd been waiting for Taylor. Now

that she was about to be his, he couldn't imagine a world in which he'd ever let her go.

At last, they reached her front door, nearly took it off the hinges in their haste to get inside, then locked it and headed through the open kitchen, dining and living rooms to the short hallway where he assumed her bedroom must be.

Her bed wasn't huge—a double as opposed to the luxurious king in his B&B suite—but he was glad for it. A smaller bed meant they'd have to stay close to each other all night long, every night, from here on out.

After so much time and distance between them— and before, when he hadn't let himself tell her how he really felt, that he loved her as so much more than just a friend—all he wanted was to be close to her. Any way, every way he could. Justin had grown up with a mother and father who loved each other deeply. He'd always known that nothing but the deepest love would be enough for him.

With Taylor, love had always been there. And now, heat was there too. Such hot, high flames jumping between their bodies as they kissed that a part of him wondered if they'd survive the night.

Standing together at the foot of her bed, he realized she was tall enough that he didn't have to bend down far to take another sweet taste of her lips—something he knew he'd never, ever get enough of.

The first time he'd set eyes on her, he'd been hit with a vision of them together, just the way they were now. His hands tangled in her hair, her mouth crushed beneath his, her heart beating fast and hard against his. All those years of waiting should have made him impatient. But now that the moment was finally here, all he wanted was to *savor*.

Savor soft kisses that ran across the sensitive skin of her neck to the hollow of her collarbone.

Savor the play of his fingers through the silk of her hair, relishing the slip and slide of the soft strands along his skin.

Savor her fresh scent, a cross between the sweet innocence of the scones she'd baked this morning and the lush sensuality of the red wine they'd tasted that afternoon.

All the while, his hands roamed her body the way he'd longed to so many times before. From the indentation of her waist to the swell of her hips, then up her arms and shoulders, strong from the work she'd done painting and gardening.

Needing to get even closer, to know how it felt to touch her bare skin—*everywhere*—he quickly lifted her T-shirt and tossed it aside, then undid the snap and zipper of her jeans so that they pooled on the wide planks of the floor. Her slip-on shoes dropped from her feet as he lifted her and laid her on the bed.

How many times had he dreamed of having her just like this? In bed, her clothes stripped away, her eyes heavy with need as she reached for him so that he could kiss her, touch her, love her. He was desperate to touch, to kiss, to finally claim her as his own—but also to stop, to stare, to memorize.

And, most of all, to give silent thanks that they'd found each other not once, but twice.

He'd been too young before to understand just how important his bond with Taylor was, but he wouldn't ever make that mistake again. He'd make the lost years up to her. Not all in one night, perhaps—although it sure as hell was worth a try.

"You're beautiful. So damned beautiful."

Joy lit her features, making her even more stunning. "So are you." She reached for him again, and he let her pull him on to the bed with her.

Levered up over her body, he kissed her again, a kiss that held a promise of wickedness. A promise her body immediately responded to as she arched her hips against his.

"Too many clothes," she said as she reached for his T-shirt.

But he'd lose control too fast if he let her strip away his clothes. Taking her hands in his, he lifted them above her head.

Her eyes were wide as she looked up at him. "Are

you going to hold me like this the whole time?"

The flare of heat in her eyes as she said it had him responding, "Do you want me to?"

She licked her lips, leaving behind a flash of wetness that couldn't be ignored. His mouth was almost over hers again when she answered, "Maybe."

There was no way to be gentle with his kisses anymore, not when he'd just learned that her sensuality ran even deeper than he'd hoped. Whatever boundaries had been between them were smashed as they passionately devoured each other's mouths.

Tonight was already the best of Justin's life. And it had only just begun.

CHAPTER EIGHT

A part of Taylor couldn't believe what she'd just said. But she knew Justin wouldn't judge her for any of her secret fantasies.

Because the truth was that she wanted to experience *everything* with him tonight. Gentle. Rough. Soft. Ragged. Sweet. Raw.

Tomorrow morning, they'd have to go back to being *just friends*—the situation was too complicated for them to do anything else. But in the dark hours until sunrise, she was more than ready to let the magic of being with Justin carry her away.

Her ex had always treated her as though she were breakable, but while she knew precisely how deep her physical limitations actually ran, she refused to act the part with Justin. She was tougher than anyone knew, even than she herself knew. These past months had tested her in so many ways, but tonight she was glad to know just how strong she really was. Strong enough not only to be ready for the extreme passion she felt in

Justin's arms—but to demand it as well.

Using the muscles she'd gained renovating her house and garden, she flipped them over on the bed so that she was sitting upright, straddling his hips. "At last, I've got you right where I want you."

"You're full of surprises, aren't you?" he said.

"I hope so." She flicked open the latch on her bra and let it drop. The widening of Justin's eyes—and the desire that flared hotter than ever—made the risk worth it.

Boldly, far more so than she'd ever been, she reached for his hands. Her breath caught in her throat as she got lost in the sensation of his fingers sliding over hers, the delicious roughness of the calluses that she guessed came from the woodworking he did to clear his mind when things in the lab got too intense.

She knew all about that kind of intensity—especially when it came to her feelings for him. And when she placed his hands over her breasts, she couldn't hold back a low moan of pleasure at how good it felt to finally know his touch in such an intimate place.

"*Taylor.*"

She heard the awe in his voice, or maybe that was just the echo of her own feelings inside her head. And when he moved his hands over her bare skin…

Oh.

God.

She couldn't keep from arching into his hands, nor could she stop her head from falling back, or her hips from moving into his. Layers of fabric still separated them—her panties and his jeans—but it was still good.

So good.

Knowing it was Justin beneath her, knowing his hands were on her bare breasts, knowing his erection was pushing into the heated vee between her legs, was better than anything she could remember. So much better that she was already on the verge of coming apart.

"Soon," he promised in a low voice, obviously reading the signs her body was giving him. "But not yet."

She couldn't process his words for several long moments, could barely even register that he'd not only spoken, but had also flipped them so that she was beneath him again.

His eyes were a dark promise of sin. "I want to feel you come for me, Taylor. Against my hands, my lips, my tongue. I want to hear you say my name. I want to hear you *beg* for me to never, ever stop loving you."

His wicked promises—and sinfully sexy demands—rocked something deep inside her. Something she'd been afraid even to acknowledge with her ex. Not just a need for satisfaction, but a *craving* for pleasure.

If she hadn't trusted Justin, she could have never admitted it. But there was almost no one she trusted more.

"Yes," she gasped. *"Please."*

And then, thank God, he was dragging her panties off, and his mouth was between her thighs. No more teasing. No more desperate anticipation. Just the shockingly wet, hot slide of his tongue over her.

She hadn't known it was possible to feel so much, to ache so deeply, or to rise so high. Especially with his hands on her breasts, doing just as much to devastate as his lips and tongue were doing between her legs.

"Justin." The tremors started as she spoke his name, coming from way down deep inside of her and radiating out with such power that she couldn't have held them in even if she'd wanted to.

She tried to get closer any way she could, but though he wasn't holding her wrists over her head anymore, he still managed to hold her right where he wanted her with his hands on her breasts and his mouth between her legs.

If she hadn't already been on the verge of detonation, knowing that she was his to pleasure any way he wanted—and that he seemed to understand exactly what she wanted without being told—sent her desire jumping even higher. Demanding *more*. More touch. More sensation. And an even higher peak to crest before she finally leaped.

Reading her mind again, his hands and mouth switched places. His lips covered her breast at the same time that his fingers circled the slick, hot skin between her legs. She opened her legs wider for him and arched up into his touch.

Her inner muscles surrounded his fingers as he made slow, steady thrusts in time to the nip of his teeth and the damp slide of his tongue at the tip of her breast.

As she rode the very edge of ecstasy, her hips were moving in an unconscious rhythm and her skin was slick with sweat. His name fell over and over from her lips, and she could hear the wonder in her own voice…along with the emotion she could no longer hold back.

"Taylor." His voice had a rough, raw edge she'd never heard before. "Look at me. I need to see you. Let me see you."

She was the one who couldn't take another second of his sensual teasing, and yet *he* sounded like the one who was begging.

"You can have anything you want." How could she promise him less? *"Anything."*

"All I've ever wanted is you."

His whispered words were the final push into bliss so breathtaking that any worries about her future, or regrets about her past, were utterly overwhelmed by the beauty of finally knowing pleasure in the arms of the man she loved.

* * *

Justin could play the last sixty seconds on repeat for the rest of his life—over and over and over and over—and he would be happy.

Happy to hear Taylor's voice go raw and ragged as she promised him *anything*.

Happy to feel her soft skin, her lithe curves, pressed hot and damp against him.

Happy to watch as emotion—and ecstasy—filled her gaze while she trusted him to give her pleasure.

With her body still quaking from her climax, he took her mouth again. Only to find her kisses even more passionate.

"More." She was reaching for his shirt again. "I need more of you." All out of patience now, this time he let her pull it up over his head. *"Wow."* She licked her lips. "You used to take your shirt off sometimes when we were outside, and it was always so hard for me not to stare."

"Stare all you want, just as long as you're planning to touch too."

"Oh yes, I'm definitely going to touch..." She reached up to run the flat of her hands over his bare chest. "And kiss…" She placed her mouth in the center of his chest, right over his heart, which was beating at hyper-speed. "Every part of you."

When she reached for his jeans, the gentle pressure of her hands over his erection was nearly enough to have him kicking off the denim in one breath and plunging into her with the next. Somehow, he got enough of a grip on himself to let her pull off the rest of his clothes. And was he ever glad he had, because within seconds of stripping him bare, she was wrapping her hand around him—and then lowering her lips to cover the same heated flesh.

Even a superhero couldn't have kept his hands from tangling in her hair, or his hips from bucking closer to her mouth, as she ran her tongue over his hard length, then took him inside.

Justin had fantasized about being with Taylor for so many years that he could barely believe this was actually happening. Not only that the girl of his dreams was loving him so openly, so joyfully. But also that he didn't have to pretend not to feel everything that he felt for her.

At long last, they were able to love each other, and it was better—infinities better—than anything he could ever have imagined.

But though she was currently making one of his hottest fantasies come true, he needed to look into her eyes, needed to hold her hands, needed to tell her with both words and actions how much she meant to him. Lifting her so that she lay on the bed again, he took her hands in his and moved over her. He loved how she immediately wrapped her legs around his waist, then rocked her hips up into his so that he could feel the hot slick of her arousal gliding over him.

Somewhere in the back of his head, a red light flashed—a warning that he was almost too far gone, too close to heaven, to heed. But no matter how much they might want to, two biology majors couldn't ignore the workings of the reproductive system.

"Protection." She blinked up at him as though trying to make sense of the word. "We need protection," he repeated.

"The bathroom. I have some condoms in a drawer." Jealousy rose up bitterly fast inside of him, even though he should be glad that she had what they needed. "Hurry," she urged, and he forced himself to move off the bed.

All but ransacking her bathroom drawers like a burglar in a rush not to get caught, he finally found the little silver packets. Grabbing a handful, he dropped all but one onto the bed. After he tore it open and tossed the empty wrapper to the floor, she put her hands over his to help him slide it on.

"*Finally.*" He threaded his hands through hers and

braced his hips against hers as he took her with a groan of pleasure that sounded more animal than human. Which was how he felt right now, utterly lost to thousands of years of pure male instinct. To have. To take. To possess. "You're mine, Taylor. *Mine.*"

He thrust deep, making her gasp as he moved over her, inside of her. Again and again, he plunged into her, running kisses over her neck, her shoulders, across the swell of her breasts and then the taut tips, where he lingered as she moaned with pleasure.

And all the while, she held tightly to his hands. Held on as she wrapped her legs even tighter around his waist. Held on while she arched and bucked against him. Held on as she went momentarily still against him and he felt the first strong pulls of her inner muscles around him.

Her name was a whisper of wonder, bliss, awe on his lips as he lifted his head to watch her shatter once more into a million beautiful pieces. And as he followed her into the brilliant blaze of fireworks, he silently vowed that nothing would ever keep them apart again.

★ ★ ★

Taylor never wanted to let Justin go. She'd never felt so good. Never been anywhere near as happy.

It turned out dreams really could come true.

For one night, at least.

But she didn't want to think about tomorrow. Until morning actually dawned, she wanted to make as many of her naughty dreams about Justin come true as she possibly could.

The naughtier the better.

"Do you want to take a bath together?"

He gave her a wonderfully wicked smile. "Hell *yes*, I want to take a bath together!"

His over-the-top enthusiasm made her laugh. It was one of the things she'd missed most during the years he'd been overseas.

"I'll go get the water heated up in the tub."

"What can I do to help?"

Taylor licked her lips, heady with the knowledge that Justin wanted her as much as she wanted him. "You can watch."

She had never been the kind of woman to use her sexual wiles on a man. Having a long-term boyfriend throughout college meant she'd never needed to. And with her ex, well, things had never really been all that sexy or exciting.

For the first time, she relished the chance to give in to the deeply sensual side of herself that she'd always kept hidden.

She relished every sway, every bounce, of her curves as she walked slowly to the oversized clawfoot tub in the corner of the room, then bent to turn on the taps. This tub had been the biggest expense of her cottage renovation, an especially big luxury considering it was nothing her customers were ever going to use. But she'd been unable to resist the thought of soaking in the tub after a long day, staring out at the stars through the large window that looked out on a private area behind her cottage.

Tonight, she was more glad than ever that she'd spent a little extra for the tub—and overjoyed that it was big enough for two.

Testing the water with her fingertips, she looked over her shoulder at Justin. Though he was lounging on the bed, his eyes held the look of a hungry predator. One who wanted to eat her up, head to toe.

God, did she ever want him to do just that. *Again.*

A new flush of desire hit her as she said, "It's ready."

"What about you?" He pushed back the covers, and she actually lost her breath at his male beauty—he was hard in all the right places. "Are you ready too?"

"Yes." She'd never known her voice could sound that breathy. That full of out-and-out lust.

The next thing she knew, he was at her side and lifting her into the tub so that he sat with his back to the far edge and she straddled him. He threaded his hands into her hair, and when he kissed her, he stole the rest of her breath away.

She never wanted to stop kissing him. Never wanted to go another day or night without touching him. Never wanted to leave his arms. Never, ever wanted this moment to end.

Again, she pushed all thoughts of morning away. Right now was all that mattered—and the memories she'd take with her would get her through the tough times to come.

By the time he let her lips go, her mouth was tingling in the most delicious way and her skin felt just the slightest bit raw from the bristles on his cheeks. "I always wondered what your five o'clock shadow felt like." She caressed his face with one hand, luxuriating in the feel of him. "It feels *wonderful*."

"All this time," he said in a voice that resonated with emotion, "we were both wanting the same thing. Each other."

Her hand stilled on his jaw. They weren't in an emotional danger zone yet, but if she wasn't careful, they would be. Of course she couldn't bury her head in the sand forever—but were a few perfect hours too much to ask? Taylor didn't want anything to spoil her fantasy, not when she needed it more than ever.

The hardest part of it all was that her heart longed as much for deep emotion as for hot sex. In a different world, where she was perfectly healthy and Justin's mother still a phone call away, Taylor would have leaped at the chance to declare her love to him—and hope that he would declare his right back.

But that wasn't the world they were living in. So she would make the most of the unexpected gift she'd been given—one sinfully sexy night with the man she loved. And she would cling to the memories long after it was over.

Stuffing down the part of herself that hated having to deflect emotion, she said, "I'm so glad we're making up for lost time tonight." She deliberately said *tonight* because she refused to lie to him about a future. "I can't wait to make up some more right now…"

She lowered her mouth to his neck, where she could feel his pulse beat steady and strong against her lips. His hands were still tangled in her hair, and as she ran kisses across his shoulders and then his chest, his fingers tightened. As though he couldn't stand the thought of letting her go.

A sob nearly rose up in her chest. Knowing she couldn't saddle Justin with her illness didn't make it any easier to accept their too rapidly fleeting hours together.

She wanted to cling to him, wanted to bury her face against his neck and stay like that forever. Instead, she worked harder than ever to push away the dark thoughts—and to focus on the fact that for the next few hours, she was the luckiest woman alive.

And about to get even luckier, if the wonderfully hard erection she was wrapping her hand around was anything to go by.

The thought made her smile. So did Justin's growl of need—and his hands coming around her waist to pull her higher.

"I need you again." He reached for a condom that she hadn't realized he'd brought over to the tub. "Now."

The water sloshed around them as they both shifted so that he could roll on protection, and then his hands were on her waist, his mouth was on hers, and she was plunging down, taking all of him at once.

The breath rushed from her lungs as he possessed her completely, driving her closer and closer to madness with every beautiful thrust.

"I can't get enough of you." He spoke the words between kisses. "I'll never be able to get enough."

She wanted to tell him it was the same for her. Wanted to blurt out how much she loved him. That she'd loved him for as long as she could remember. But she couldn't confess any of it, couldn't live with herself if she gave him her heart tonight and then took it all away tomorrow.

Her body, however, wouldn't listen to the rational voices inside her head or be held back by what the doctors said. And as they made love, every part of her that could touch Justin, that could pleasure and be pleasured, went all in.

Water splashed.

Hands stroked and caressed.

Mouths tasted and nipped.

And raw moans of pleasure filled her room.

Justin drove her higher and higher and higher, the rest of the world disappearing. After driving each other into frenzied ecstasy, at last they collapsed together, lungs heaving, clinging to each other so tightly that it was difficult to draw breath.

"That was unbelievable. Best day of my life." Justin stroked the wet hair back from her face. "You're going to run me ragged."

She gazed into his beautiful face. "If you don't think you can keep up…"

His grin stole her heart, just like it always had. "We Morrisons are known for our stamina."

She raised an eyebrow. "Really?"

"Is that doubt I hear?"

Knowing he'd always thrived on a challenge, she said, "There's only one way to prove me wrong."

He had her out of the tub and bouncing onto her bed in the blink of an eye. They were both still soaking wet as they tangled mouths and limbs again. And if she couldn't help but wish for more—for just as much emotion as pleasure—she reminded herself that even this was more than she'd ever hoped to have with Justin.

And she would never regret their night together as long as she lived.

CHAPTER NINE

Justin woke the next morning alone in Taylor's bed. He'd much rather have had her in his arms, but she had a job to do, one that included feeding her guests.

He put on his jeans and T-shirt, then went looking for her. He found her in the kitchen with little Sophia and Addison sitting on stools stuffing fresh blueberry muffins into their mouths. Grinning like a fool, he went to say good morning and give her a kiss, but she sidestepped him at the last second. And she barely smiled back.

"I just pulled the muffins out of the oven if you want one."

Trying to convince himself that her voice didn't sound stilted—and that even if it did, it was only natural for things to be a little awkward between them this morning, at least until they had a chance to talk—he grabbed a muffin. But he wasn't hungry any-more...and wouldn't be until he made absolutely sure that last night had been just as good for Taylor as it had been for him. Especially now that in the light of day, he couldn't help but rewind back to that moment in the tub when it seemed as though she hadn't wanted the two of them to talk about anything more than sex. He'd chalked it up to her being as physically hungry for him as he was for her.

Had he been wrong?

He'd been so sure that last night had solidified their connection on every level, from friendship to love and everything in between. But he'd made that mistake once before, after their kiss in college—the kiss that had torn their friendship to shreds.

No, he thought with a firm shake of his head. Things were different now. They hadn't been drunk last night. She didn't have a boyfriend. And they weren't kids anymore. They were adults who knew their own minds and hearts. She wouldn't have slept with him, wouldn't have given herself to him so openly, so fully, if she hadn't wanted to love him the way he wanted to love her.

No amount of reasoning with himself could stop him from wanting to pull her out of the kitchen and make sure everything was okay. But he knew better than to take her away from her job, of course.

Frustration rode him as Sophia and Addison's parents walked in. "We can get the little ones out of here if they're disturbing you," Katie Belmont said to Taylor, giving Justin a smile that he only barely managed to return.

"I love the kids keeping me company while I make breakfast," Taylor replied with a smile. One that was a million times bigger than the one she'd given him a few minutes ago. "You've been really helpful, haven't you?" she said to the children.

"We have!" Sophia pointed to a couple of messy piles of chocolate chips, which were slightly smeared, as though someone had licked them before putting them down. "Taylor needed us to measure the chocolate chips for cookies," she told her mother in a voice full of proud importance.

Justin made a mental note not to eat that batch of cookies, even as he appreciated Taylor's willingness to let her young guests help. His mother had been the same way when Justin and his siblings were little. She'd never been upset by dropped bags of flour or broken eggs. On the contrary, she made them all laugh even more whenever they made messy mistakes. And she never, ever called them *mistakes*.

Now, he refused to call his night with Taylor a mistake. No matter what was going on inside her head today, he knew with utter certainty that making love had been right. For both of them.

Last night, he'd finally let loose his desire for her. This morning, he would do the same with words of love. Words that he hoped would wipe away any regret she might be feeling.

"How was your night?" Taylor asked her guests.

"Really great," Brent Belmont replied. "Your restaurant suggestions have been spot-on."

"And we loved walking through town after dinner," his wife added.

"And the ice cream was awesome!" Addison rubbed his tummy. "Can we go back today?"

"You bet," said his mother with a grin before turning back to Taylor. "What about you? How was your evening? I hope you didn't work too hard."

Taylor's cheeks immediately flushed a deep rose. Just the way they had when Justin had been stroking her skin, pressing kisses along the swell of her breasts, and driving her to climax with his body inside of hers.

"I didn't work at all," she said with a little shake of her head. She licked her lips, then added, "My night was good."

Good?

"I had the best night of my life," he interjected. No one had asked him, but Justin had no intention of holding in the truth.

The Belmonts' eyebrows went up. "What did you do?" Brent asked. "Sounds like we should follow your example tonight."

"Actually, we both just stayed right here," Taylor

replied with a laugh—one that he knew for a fact was forced—before he could say anything else. "Pizza delivery under the stars in Napa Valley," she added with a smile. "Nothing better, right?"

Katie nodded. "Honestly, I'm not sure there is. Brent and I can't stop looking at real estate flyers. It would be such a dream to live here."

"It would be so lovely if you moved to St. Helena!" Taylor said, clearly excited about the idea. "We could talk more about what it's like to live here, as opposed to being a tourist, over breakfast if you'd like. Food should be ready in about ten minutes."

"I'm going to head out for a run," Justin said. "Don't wait on breakfast for me."

His tone was brusque enough that everyone had to be wondering what his problem was. But he wouldn't be able to sit at the table and keep a pleasant conversation going while his insides twisted up with every second that Taylor wouldn't look him in the eye. Going for a punishing run would be the only way to keep from force-feeding the Belmont family so they'd leave him and Taylor alone to talk.

★ ★ ★

An hour later, he came back to find the breakfast table cleared and no sign of the family of four. His T-shirt was soaked—he hadn't run that fast since he raced the mile on the track team in high school—but he headed straight for the kitchen, where he hoped to find Taylor. Alone, this time.

"Hey." He saw her standing at the kitchen sink, still not looking at him. "Is everything okay?"

It was a tip-of-the-iceberg question. One that barely scratched the surface of what he really wanted to ask. But he didn't want to make the mistake of freaking out completely on the morning after if it turned out that there was nothing to freak out about.

"I don't know if it is," she replied in a soft voice.

He'd always appreciated her honesty. She never answered a question unless she was certain about it. This morning, though, her honesty was a punch straight to his gut.

"Talk to me." He shut off the faucet and grabbed her wet hands, turning her to face him. "Last night seemed perfect. But if it was just that way for me, and not for you, you need to tell me."

"It *was* perfect," she said, her words spoken in such an intense voice that he knew she meant it. Only, instead of looking overjoyed about it, she pressed her lips together. "But—"

"You don't have to worry," he said. "I know I was a player in college, but that was only because I couldn't have you. Now that we're together, I don't want anyone else. I've never wanted anyone but you."

"You can't want me." She looked utterly panicked as she yanked her hands from his. "We can't be together."

Again, he was ready to counter her worries. "I know we'll have to deal with the long-distance stuff for a while, but I won't be in Germany forever. I was thinking it probably won't be too hard to open a lab here and find scientists who would be more than happy to live in the wine country."

"That's not it." She looked pale again, the same shade she'd been when she collapsed on the stairs.

"Are you feeling sick?" He practically carried her over to the stools the kids had been sitting on earlier. Was she coming down with the flu? He hated seeing her unwell, but at least that would explain why she was acting so strangely this morning.

Instead of answering him, she said, "I can't give you what you need."

He grabbed her hands again. "You always have, Taylor. Right from the first moment we met, I knew." Her eyes were glassy with tears about to fall. "Talk to me. Tell me what's wrong. You don't have to hide anything from me. You never have. Whatever it is, I can take it." Even if she told him that making love last night had been a mistake, that she didn't love him, he'd somehow listen, somehow deal with the enormous blow without screwing up their friendship again.

She stared into his eyes, unspeaking, for a long moment. He saw love, he swore it. So if that wasn't the problem, then what was?

Finally, she spoke. "I have a rare, fast-moving type of polycystic kidney disease."

* * *

"How the hell can you have PKD when neither of your parents have it?" Justin's voice boomed through the kitchen, so loudly that it might have shaken the windows had Taylor not recently replaced them with double panes.

Taylor wasn't surprised by his response. It was the same one she'd had—straight-up, hard-headed, science-based denial. She'd even tried to argue with the doctor. Which was when he'd given her a comprehensive tour of autosomal recessive polycystic kidney disease and then walked her through every detail of her lab results to show her how she fit all the markers. He'd encouraged her to get a second opinion, and by the time the second set of lab results came in, she'd had to accept the truth.

"With autosomal recessive PKD," she said, "both parents can be carriers and pass it on to their children without ever having it themselves." Knowing Justin was one of the few people who would understand what she was talking about, she further explained, "It's associated with a group of congenital fibrocystic syndromes. Mutations in the PKHD1 cause ARPKD. Normally, it's diagnosed during infancy or early childhood. But in some rare cases, it isn't detected until much later in life. We read about it in our *Human Anatomy and Physiology* textbook."

"I don't give a damn about what it said in our textbook!"

Her heart felt like it would break into a million pieces from the utter devastation on his face.

"All I care about is you," he said. "How many doctors have you seen?"

"Too many." With many, many more on the horizon, unfortunately.

"There's still a chance they're wrong."

"No, there isn't." She couldn't allow him any false hope. "I've been through my lab results a million times. My doctors are right. And actually," she forced herself to say, "I'm lucky they found it before things got really bad."

"*Lucky?*" He swore, a vicious rip of words. Oddly, it actually helped her to hear them. They were all the same words that she wanted to scream herself, but hadn't because she'd been so busy trying to hold it together for her parents. And she'd had to keep a clear head as she'd made plans to open her B&B.

"Why the hell didn't you tell me? And don't say it's

because I was too busy with my lab research. I should have been here right after you got the diagnosis to help you deal with it, any way I could."

"I know you would have jumped on the next plane and been here." She would have done the same for him, and the truth was that she felt ashamed for keeping it from him this long. But she didn't want to make excuses, not to the one person who mattered most. Which meant she needed to admit the truth instead. "Telling people makes it real." All of the light that their lovemaking had filled her with the night before—bright, wonderful warmth that she'd need to cling to in the future—felt as though it was draining away, letting the darkness back in. "So much more real than I want it to be. I know that sounds weak—"

"Not weak. Human." He stopped his furious pacing and moved to her side, putting his arms around her. "I understand why you didn't tell me before, but I'm going to be really upset if you keep anything else from me. And I won't let you use your diagnosis to push me away either."

She shook her head against his chest. "That's not what I'm doing."

"Like hell it isn't."

He was clearly furious and had every right to his feelings. But so did she.

"You've lost enough already." She wanted to take

the comfort he offered and wrap herself up in it. But she loved him too much to take anything more from him than he'd already given when his mother was sick. She'd do whatever it took to protect him from more pain. Even if it meant giving up his love. "I can't stand the thought of being one more thing you lose."

"You won't be."

She'd seen the way he'd reacted when she said, *You've lost enough already.* He'd been unable to hold back his grief at losing his mother, the lingering pain that he'd told her felt like a two-by-four across his chest.

His father had been destroyed by his mother's death. Justin had always said he wouldn't wish that kind of pain on his worst enemy. Neither would she.

"Of course, I hope I have a really long, full life," she said in a soft voice. "But neither of us can get away with trying to ignore the scientific facts. And the fact is that without a transplant—or even with one—I can't guarantee anything."

"Love doesn't come with guarantees," he insisted. "I love you, and I know you love me too."

"I do." More than anything else, she realized she needed him to know that, even if it didn't mean they could be together. "I love you, Justin. I've always loved you."

"Then let me be with you. As more than a friend.

Let me help you figure this out, as a team, as your partner."

"No." She forced herself out of his arms. "I already told you—I won't let you go down this road again. Because if the worst happens—"

"Goddammit, Taylor! I won't let that happen."

She knew he would move heaven and earth for her if he could. But it had taken him six long years to even begin to climb out of his grief over losing his mother.

"Please." She didn't want to cry, but she couldn't stop the tears from coming. "I don't want to fight. Not with you. Not with my best friend, especially when I haven't gotten to be with you for so long."

He tugged her tightly into his arms, and she buried her face in his neck, breathing him in. "I don't want to fight either," he said. "But that doesn't mean I'm giving up."

She knew he wouldn't back down easily. It was one of the things she loved most about him—that he always fought for what he believed in. No matter how hard, no matter how long the fight.

If only they weren't fighting on opposite sides.

There was a knock on the kitchen door. "Taylor, it's Angie," her friend called from the other side. "I hope I'm not interrupting. I just wanted to bring by the new goat's milk and cheddar cheeses you asked for. Do you want me to leave them in the dining room for you?"

Taylor quickly wiped the wetness from her cheeks and made herself move out of Justin's arms. "Come on in, Angie. This is my friend Justin. He's visiting for a few days."

For a moment, she was certain that he would correct her. She wasn't sure which part he'd jump on first—that she'd called him her *friend* rather than *boyfriend*, or that he was going to be around for only a few days.

Fortunately, he simply shook Angie's hand. "Sorry to say hello and run, but I should get into the shower. Taylor and I have a big day ahead of us, and I don't want to waste any of it."

She already knew exactly the form their big day was going to take. He was going to keep trying to convince her that they should be together, her disease be damned, and she was going to have to keep resisting the one thing she wanted most in the world.

The worst part of it all, though? That even going around and around on such a difficult subject with him would be better than anything she could do with anyone else. Even when things were bad with Justin, they were good.

That's what a goner she was, and had always been, when it came to her best friend.

"He's cute," Angie said after he left the kitchen.

"Just friends, you say?"

Taylor met Angie at a local business owners' networking event last month and was thrilled to have made a friend so quickly. But the last thing she was up to this morning was dishing about her endless crush on Justin.

"It's complicated."

"Good complicated or bad complicated?"

"Both."

"If you need to talk, you know where I am."

"Thanks, Angie. I may need to do just that in a few days." After Justin went back to Germany, something Taylor couldn't even think about without feeling as though her heart would break.

But she refused to let herself get weepy. The sun was shining. The flowers were blooming. And she'd just had a night of unforgettably great sex with her best friend. For now, that was enough to keep a smile on her face.

It had to be.

CHAPTER TEN

Justin brought his laptop downstairs and set it up on the dining table, barely able to keep his hands from shaking. He hadn't lost it, hadn't fallen apart, since the day his mother passed away, but he felt damned close to that edge right now.

"I'd like to see everything the doctors have given you about the disease." The letters P, K, and D felt like poison on his tongue now, so he did what he could to avoid saying them. "And your lab results too, if you wouldn't mind showing them to me."

"Of course I'll show you everything." Taylor went into the small room off the kitchen that she used as her office and pulled several thick folders from the bottom of the filing cabinet. But she didn't give them to him immediately. "Promise me you won't freak out when you start reading."

"Too late." Even if he tried to tell her comforting lies, she'd see right through them. "I need to know what we're up against."

"Not *we*, Justin. You've already fought one battle for your mother. You don't have to fight mine too."

"Like hell I don't." He all but ripped the folders from her hands. When her eyes went wide, he inwardly cursed himself. "I'm sorry." The effort it took to keep himself together was almost more than he could bear as he looked at the woman he loved. The woman he wanted to spend the rest of his life with. The woman who had just told him about her diagnosis. "I just keep thinking that the sooner I start combing through everything, the sooner I'll find a solution."

"I knew that's what you'd do." She wrapped her arms around him, the folders between them like a bag of bricks. "I just don't want you to be upset when you don't find one." Too quickly, she kissed his cheek and stepped back. "I've got some errands to do and then some business to take care of in my office. We can talk more when I get back, okay?"

He wouldn't let her go without a kiss. A real one this time.

Her mouth was soft beneath his. And oh so sweet. Especially when she started kissing him back. A kiss that told him everything she felt for him, even if she thought she needed to push him away for his own good.

Before she walked away, however, she said, "I haven't changed my mind about what I said earlier."

"Neither have I."

He would have given her another kiss to prove his point, but she slipped away before he could. As though she hadn't yet realized that he'd stop at nothing to persuade her not only to be with him, but to also let him support her in her fight against her disease.

A fight he needed to arm himself for by being as informed as possible.

He began with her test results, his scientific mind whirring into overdrive as he read. Two hours later, when he finished the final set of reports in her files, he knew more about PKD than he'd ever thought he would.

And he was also more frightened than he'd ever been.

The literature made it clear that many people with the dominant PKD gene lived long lives with the disease. The majority, in fact. But for patients with autosomal recessive PKD…

No, damn it! He wouldn't let himself lose traction in helping Taylor by getting stuck in dark thoughts and dangerous statistics. No matter what, he needed to stay calm and clear-headed. Otherwise, he wouldn't be a help, he'd be a hindrance.

She came through the door carrying a large box, and he leaped from his chair to take it from her. "You shouldn't be carrying that."

She gave him a look like he was nuts. "It's just ears of corn. I carry heavier things all the time."

"Don't." Realizing too late that the word had shot from his lips like a bullet, he ran a hand through his hair. "Sorry." He had a feeling he was going to be apologizing a lot, like a panicked bull rampaging out of control in a china shop.

"I take it you read through everything?" she asked.

He nodded, bringing the box of fresh corn through to the kitchen. "Do you want me to help you shuck these?"

"That would be great," she said with a smile clearly meant to show that she wasn't upset with him for freaking out that she was carrying something heavy.

As he tore at the corn husks while he continued to mentally process everything he'd read during the past two hours, his jaw clenched so tight that it started to pop. He would have much preferred shredding her doctors' reports to pieces.

"I'll go toss the garbage bag so we have room for all of this." She had to shimmy around the island to get by him and ended up bumping into the corner of it.

"Careful!"

"Justin," she said, her voice carefully modulated, "I understand that all of this is a huge, horrible shock to you. But you need to stop freaking out."

"Stop?" He gripped the ear of corn he was holding

so tightly that juice from the raw kernels started to run through his fingers. "How the hell am I supposed to stop freaking out? And how the hell could you not have told me before we made love? I could have hurt you!"

"You would never have hurt me."

"Of course I wouldn't have done it on purpose." The dozens of case studies he'd just read swam together inside his head. "But if I had jolted you the wrong way, or put too much pressure on your kidneys—"

"Making love with you was the best I've felt in months!" Her words stopped his in their tracks. "Don't you dare take last night away from me or make me feel guilty about it."

Softening his voice, he said, "I can't stand the thought that I could have hurt you."

"You didn't." She moved into his arms, and he held on to her as tightly as he dared. "You won't."

"If only we could be sure." He breathed in her fresh scent, letting it fill him up. "I just want to be sure."

Sure that she'd have a long and healthy life. Sure that they could share the life he'd dreamed of together. One full of kids and grandkids and love and laughter. And *time*.

Before she could respond, the front door opened and voices called, "Taylor? Justin?"

Taylor's eyes grew big, and she stepped out of his arms. "That sounds like Drew and Ashley." She hurried out of the kitchen to greet their unexpected guests. "What a lovely surprise," he heard her say right before she brought his brother and his fiancée through the door.

Justin gave them each a hug, noting that they were both glowing with pre-wedding happiness. Normally, it would be good to see them on the spur of the moment like this, but nothing was normal right now.

"Any chance we can convince you guys to come with us to Sullivan Winery to check out the final wedding preparations?" Ashley asked. But then she paused and took a careful look at their faces. "Of course, if you're in the middle of something, we understand."

Ashley had always had a knack for sensing when someone was hurting. It was part of the reason she and Drew had initially connected. She'd been invited to join Drew's concert tour a little more than five years ago to conduct research for a master's degree on the music business. Though Drew's music career had looked like it was going from strength to strength, the truth that he'd kept from all of them was that he wasn't happy. Ashley had seen through the walls he'd put up, and she hadn't hesitated to help him figure out what changes he needed to make to really enjoy making music again. Drew had done the same for her when he'd shown her how talented she really was, and he'd also helped to repair her relationship with her parents. Since then, they'd lived happily ever after—with their wedding this weekend making it official.

At present, Drew had his arm around Ashley's waist. He obviously couldn't stand for her to be anywhere but pressed closely against him. They were the most in-love people Justin knew, apart from Sean and Serena. Justin's parents had been that much in love too.

His chest clenched tight as he looked at Taylor. He wanted to hold her just as closely—and know that he'd never need to let her go. Which was why he didn't think it was a good idea to go off with his brother and Ashley right now. The two of them needed to hash everything out, no matter how tough the hashing-out was.

"Actually, maybe now isn't—" Justin began, but Taylor quickly cut in.

"We were just getting some corn shucked for cornbread and chowder, but that can absolutely wait until after we get a sneak peek at your wedding venue."

"And miss out on chowder and cornbread?" Drew looked seriously disappointed. He was always up for the chance to eat great home-cooked food.

"How about we take the muffins I made this morning with us to the winery?" She handed one to Ashley and another to Drew. "I've got to be back to put out afternoon tea for my guests, but that should still leave us plenty of time."

Drew's eyes all but rolled back in his head as he shoved half the muffin into his mouth. *"Mmff ggdd."*

What would Drew's millions of fans think of him if they could see him now, with crumbs and unintelligible sounds coming out of his mouth? But Justin already knew. They'd love him more.

Just like there was nothing that Taylor could say or do that would make Justin love her less.

★ ★ ★

Visiting Sullivan Winery affirmed to Taylor yet again that she had made the right decision to move to Napa Valley. The landscape was beyond beautiful, and the sky was so blue it almost didn't seem real. She'd never be able to look out over the rolling hills covered in lush grapevines without them taking her breath away.

She was glad that Ashley and Drew had shown up unexpectedly. Being forced to stop thinking about her diagnosis for a little while was exactly what Justin needed. She wanted him to relax and enjoy his time off, not waste the rest of the week hunched over a computer on a desperate goose chase for a cure.

"The weather looks like it will be perfect this weekend," Nicola Sullivan said to Ashley and Drew with a cheerful smile. "Just as we discussed earlier, we're planning to set up the chairs for the ceremony over there." She pointed to a large section of manicured green lawn and rosebushes between the tasting room and the vines. "We'll set up everything for the reception just around the corner."

Taylor was having a hard time not being star struck as Nicola led them around to the other side of the building. She knew all of Nicola's songs—which had been written and released under her stage name, Nico—by heart. Sure, Drew was also a massive music star, but Taylor had known him before he hit it big, so he felt like a brother to her. Whereas Nicola was even more sparkling and beautiful and captivating in person than she was in concert and in her videos. Taylor had met Nicola and her husband, Marcus, a little more than five years ago when Drew and Nicola had done a combined acoustic tour together, but it was still hard to act completely normal around her.

"That's quite a girl crush you've got," Justin teased her in a low voice, obviously having noted her mute adoration, broken up by only a couple of awkward giggles when Nicola had tried to talk with her.

"Shhh." She felt her cheeks flush, mortified that Nicola might have heard him. But then she had to whisper back, "She's just so amazing."

"You're not the only one who thinks so." He nodded toward Marcus Sullivan, who was laughing at something his wife had said, a look of all-consuming love on his handsome face.

"They are definitely giving Ashley and Drew some serious competition for the Most Perfect Couple in the World Award," she said with a little sigh.

"So could we." His statement stopped her in her tracks, just the way she was certain he'd intended. The others were continuing around the corner of the building, leaving them alone as he said, "Let me love you, Taylor. And let yourself love me back. I know things aren't easy right now, but that's what love is, isn't it? Sticking together in good times and bad. In sickness and in health."

Her heart clenched as he all but made his vows to her right then and there. He'd always been her best friend, but he was right in saying he'd make an even better boyfriend. She wanted to be with him so badly—wanted it more than anything she'd ever wanted before.

But wouldn't it be selfish to fall into his arms when she was such a mess? She had to be realistic, even if she hated what reality held for her. For them.

"I can't stand the thought of putting you through the sick watch again. You read my charts, so you know that dating me would be like dating a ticking time bomb."

"Be with me, Taylor." Determination radiated from him.

"Have you heard anything I've said? Do you understand at all where I'm coming from, that I only want to protect you?"

"I heard every word. But it doesn't change a thing. I love you. I've always loved you and I always will. You don't need to protect me. I promise you that I'm strong enough to take whatever comes. Strong enough to be there for you. Strong enough to help you with anything you need help with."

How could she possibly resist him when he opened his arms to her? No one could have, unless they were made of ice.

"I know exactly how strong you are." For a moment, she let herself lean into his strength as she rested her cheek on his chest and wrapped her arms around him. But she knew what caring for, worrying about, and researching cures for his mother, all while putting on a brave face, had done to him. How it had almost turned him into a shell of himself. That was precisely why she hadn't thought she could ask him to be strong for her too. Still trying to be strong, trying to do what she'd been so convinced was the right thing for him, she forced herself to pull back a couple of inches. "But I won't ever be able to forgive myself if I end up hurting you."

"You're not going to hurt me."

He sounded so certain that she almost believed he could make it so. And when he lowered his mouth to hers, she felt as though the passion and the emotion in their kiss just might be the magic ingredients she needed to make her wishes come true.

"Will you let me love you, Taylor?" He held her face in his hands, holding her heart just as tightly, as he gazed into her eyes with deep emotion. "Will you let yourself love me back? No matter what hurdles we have to face, now or in the future?"

She had tried to keep him safe, but she knew deep in her heart that in the end, she would never be able to keep in, or hold back, her love for him. Not now that it had finally spilled forth last night in the most beautiful way possible. She couldn't promise anything when it came to her health, but she could promise him this: "I will let you love me. And I will let myself love you too. I want to be with you, Justin. It's what I've always wanted."

They were kissing when Ashley and Drew came back around the building. Justin's arms tightened around her when he saw them, but he needn't have worried that she was going to pull away again.

Giving him up was the very last thing she wanted.

Guilt at the thought that she shouldn't have been so quick to fall into his arms—that she should have tried harder to protect him from future pain—pulled at her as Ashley and Drew beamed at them.

"Aha!" Drew said with a wide grin as he wagged his finger between them. "I knew something was going on in the kitchen this morning." His eyebrows moved up and down in an exaggerated manner. "You two are finally getting it on, aren't you?"

Taylor felt her face go up in flames as Ashley smacked her fiancé's shoulder. "Drew!"

But Drew looked positively gleeful. "We've all been waiting *forever* for the two of you to see the light. To do the horizontal tango. To bump fuzzies. To make a bedspring symphony."

Ashley clamped her hand over Drew's mouth, giving Taylor and Justin an apologetic look even as the corners of her own mouth were twitching with a smile she was barely holding back. "Sorry that my husband-to-be has no manners."

He nipped at her hand, before saying, "Good thing you love that about me." Then he gave her a seriously hot kiss.

"What I came to ask before Drew went out of his way to get a rise out of both of you," Ashley continued in a slightly breathless voice when he let her go, "is, would you mind coming to look at the guest house with me, Taylor? It's where I'll be getting ready on the morning of the wedding, and my brain is so overfull with details already that I'm afraid I might miss something I'll need."

"I'd be happy to come take a look with you."

And she was even happier to be able to give Justin a kiss, rather than silently long for one the way she used to. Their kiss was soft and sweet and set dozens of butterflies loose inside of her. If only the shadow of guilt—and the weight of her worries about the future—would give up their grip on her, everything would be perfect.

But even though *perfect* wasn't in the cards for her, that didn't mean she couldn't appreciate every wonderful moment she and Justin had together now. If anything, she appreciated them even more.

★ ★ ★

"Finally," Drew said as he threw an arm around Justin's shoulders, "you've got the girl of your dreams."

A server came out of the tasting room with a tray of champagne flutes. "Here are several vintages that Marcus and Nicola suggest you taste so that you can make your final selections for this weekend."

"Perfect timing," Drew declared. "My brother and I have plenty to celebrate."

They were sitting on outdoor chairs in the shade of a large oak when Drew picked up a glass and held it out to Justin in a toast. "To both of us snaring the women we were meant to be with."

Justin clinked his glass with Drew's, but barely took a sip. Holding Taylor in the middle of the vineyard, hearing her say that she loved him and that she wanted to be with him, meant more to him than anything else ever had. He'd never felt so high.

Or so low, when he thought about how much time he'd wasted. "How could I have been such an idiot not to tell her how I feel years ago?"

"No point in worrying about the past," Drew said. "You've got the future to look forward to."

The future. Justin had read all the statistics about the life-spans of PKD patients—the progress the scientific community had made with dialysis and kidney transplants was impressive. But he wanted guarantees, damn it. For the hundredth time in the past hour, he went back through everything he'd read before leaving the B&B.

Drew frowned when Justin didn't immediately agree that his future was all roses and sunshine now that Taylor was his. "I'm pretty sure you have everything you've ever wanted now," his brother remarked. "So why aren't you skipping through the vineyards with cartoon hearts floating around your head?"

Justin hated to break Taylor's confidence, but he needed to talk this through with someone. His father, though brilliant, was out of the question. Something told Justin there was a chance Dad might even agree with Taylor's concerns about getting too close—if only to try to protect his son from any harm.

When the truth was that the only thing that would truly devastate Justin was living without her.

"You're right," he said to his brother. "This should be the best day of my life. After all these years of loving Taylor but not being able to tell her or show her, and not knowing if she felt the same way, my mind is blown to find out I'm not the only one who has those feelings."

"So then I'll ask again—where are the cartoon hearts?"

"She's been diagnosed with PKD."

Drew frowned. "What the hell is PKD? It sounds like the name of a bad metal band."

"I wish it were." Justin quickly explained the parameters of the disease to his brother, who looked shell-shocked by the news. "Unless she gets a kidney—and preferably from a live donor—things are likely to get really rough, really fast."

"Donate yours." Drew said it as though it was the most obvious thing in the world.

"I would, in a heartbeat." Of course, Justin had already thought of that. "But she was so intent on shielding me from her disease that she didn't even want us to be together. How the heck am I going to convince her to take one of my kidneys?"

"Do you think she'd be more open to taking one of mine?"

Justin had never been a crier. Even when his mother had been sick, he'd pushed tears away with medical books and scientific research up until the very end. But hearing his brother offer to donate a kidney to Taylor without even a moment's hesitation—

Sometimes a guy couldn't stop himself from choking up.

"Thanks, Drew." Emotion at the sacrifice his brother was willing to make made his voice rough. "But if Taylor's going to have a piece of someone inside her, it's going to be me."

As brothers who had shared endless dirty jokes as kids, they both had to laugh at the double meaning of his words, but it was muted humor.

"I'm going to tell her I want to be tested to see if I'm a match." Now that Justin had made up his mind, he was unwavering. "And if I'm a compatible donor, I'm not going to let her say no."

"Whatever you need," his brother said, "just let me know."

Justin looked in the direction the women had gone. "I've got to make a couple of calls to get the ball rolling ASAP. Could you distract Ashley and Taylor in case they come back before I'm done?"

He knew without a shadow of a doubt that since Taylor had only just come on board with dating him, she *really* wasn't going to be happy about him wanting to be her donor. If she overheard his calls to the transplant center before he had a chance to talk her around to the idea, it wouldn't help his case one bit to debate it in front of Drew and Ashley.

"No problem," Drew agreed.

Justin knew a couple of scientists at the University of California at Davis, which was not only less than an hour away, but also had one of the best kidney-transplant centers in the nation. Thankfully, they were more than happy to connect him with the transplant team, and dropping their names got him an appointment first thing the next morning for the blood tests he and Taylor would have to have to check their compatibility for a transplant.

"Nice work," Drew said when he put his phone down. "Perfect timing too. Looks like Ash and Taylor are just heading back."

As he watched the woman he'd always been crazy about laugh with Drew's fiancée, Justin pushed away every ounce of doubt, letting only hope and love remain. He and Taylor had always been the perfect match for each other. They just needed to be a perfect match again so that he could give her his kidney.

He refused to accept any other possibility.

CHAPTER ELEVEN

As Taylor got into Justin's car, she felt much more relaxed than she had an hour ago, thanks to the fresh air, beautiful scenery, and laughter with good friends.

She had just reached for Justin's hand when he turned to her from the driver's seat. "We've got an appointment for blood tests tomorrow morning with the transplant team at UC Davis."

Wait, what did he just say? He wanted to donate a kidney to her?

Of everything she'd thought they'd be talking about on their drive back to her B&B, this was nowhere on the list. After all, she'd only just wrapped her head around dating him when they both knew her health was in rapid decline. But to let him give her one of his kidneys?

Had he hit his head on something when she and Ashley had left to check out the guest house?

Taylor's brain—and her heart—were full of so many conflicting thoughts and emotions that, instead of being able to clearly break down all the reasons he couldn't do this for her, she said, "I can't go tomorrow morning. I have to make breakfast for guests."

As if Justin would reply, *Well, sure, if you need to make breakfast, then why don't we both forget about my offer to donate a kidney to you.*

"Maddie is going to come up from the city to take care of breakfast and anything else you need done while we're at Davis."

Taylor knew she should be grateful. A live donor had the potential to make all the difference in the world, but the waiting list had over 100,000 people on it—and it could take seven to ten years for her to make it to the top.

But she was already terrified of hurting Justin simply by getting sicker and sicker due to her disease. She couldn't imagine the depths of her grief, her guilt, if he ended up being a compatible donor and then something happened to him during surgery, or after.

Again, however, she couldn't think in a line straight enough to say anything rational. Instead, what came out was, "I can't believe you arranged all this behind my back while I was with Ashley."

"I'm not going to apologize. Not for wanting to donate one of my kidneys to you. And not for loving you either." To back up his words, he leaned over and kissed her—a kiss that sent just as many zings of pleasure through her as his offer to help her in the most profound way possible had sent zings of confusion and conflict through her. "I'm not going to lose you now, Taylor. Especially when I know that you love me and you know that I love you. I'm in this with you all the way, no matter what. So as long as there's even a ghost of a chance that I can donate to you, I'll take it."

Forcing herself to take some deep breaths, she worked to bend her wayward thoughts back into straight lines. Justin obviously wasn't going to back down about the two of them getting blood tests to see if he was a match. And the truth was that she would have insisted on the very same thing if she had been in his shoes.

Finally, she said, "I'll go and get tested with you."

But all the while, she'd hold on to the hope that Justin wouldn't be a compatible donor. Because if he was, she'd have to make the most difficult decision of her life.

★ ★ ★

For the next several hours, Taylor was busy serving and then clearing up afternoon tea. A new couple checked in, and the Belmonts, who had already met with a local Realtor, wanted Taylor's opinion on the properties they'd seen. Her mother called a couple of times, but she'd let both calls go through to voice mail, instead sending a text that said, *Super busy, but doing good. Will call you tomorrow.* Her day had been such a roller-coaster ride that she didn't think she could pull off a normal conversation with her mom just yet—not when she was certain that Caroline Cardenes would instantly know what her daughter had been doing, and who she'd been doing it with, from nothing more than the sound of her voice.

Unfortunately, Justin Morrison had always been a tricky subject with her mother...

If only Caroline could see how good he was with Sophie and Addison as they sold lemonade and cookies on the sidewalk at a stand he'd hammered together from some leftover lumber at the back of her property. He was such a natural with kids. And she was happy that the Belmont children had distracted him from his computer. All too soon, she and Justin would be back in the deep end at the transplant center tomorrow morning.

After the lemonade stand sold out of its goodies, the kids went off to dinner in town with their parents. She and Justin ate chowder and cornbread, and once they'd finished eating, they sat out in her yard, with only the crickets for company and the moon shining full and round in the night sky.

Anyone looking at the couple holding hands in the

moonlight would think everything was perfect. They would never be able to guess at the turmoil roiling just below the surface—or the fact that Taylor's day had been full not only of more love than she'd ever known it was possible to feel, but also more confusion that she ever wanted to have to face.

Last night, she'd let herself be swept away in the magic of being with Justin at last, the heady romance of his kisses, the sinfully sweet culmination of years of longing. Tonight, she needed Justin's love to wrap around her and fill up her reserves. Reserves that were running perilously low.

Before she could say a word, he was pulling her up from her seat. "I can't wait to make love with you again. Not another second."

"I can't wait either," she replied, relief filling every word.

She should have guessed that he would be feeling the same way, should have known that for all his confident words about helping her win her battles, his reserves would be just as low as hers.

Hand in hand, they all but ran through the garden to her cottage. Last night, when the floodgates had opened, she'd let her body soar, but she'd tried to keep hold of her heart.

Tonight, her heart was in charge. Where it went, her body would follow.

Once they were inside, she leaped into his arms, kissing him with all the love that filled her.

Lost in his kiss, it took her longer than it should have to realize how gently he was holding her. Too gently. As though she might break at any moment.

"Justin." She slid down his body, no longer afraid to give free rein to her sensuality. Not with him. "You don't need to treat me like porcelain." She followed up her words with a rough tug at his shirt, pulling it out of his jeans and over his head. "I don't want you to hold anything back," she urged as she deftly undid his belt and zipper. "I want you to show me how much you want me."

"So damned much." He growled the words against her lips as he captured her jaw in his hands and held her captive with his kiss. And yet, when he lifted his mouth from hers, she saw the same concern in his eyes that she felt in his hands on her hips. "But I need to be careful with you."

She understood why he felt that way. After all, the shadow of fear had underlain nearly every moment of every day since she'd collapsed at the town hall. Until last night, when Justin had swept away everything but pleasure for a few precious hours.

There were going to be countless big battles to fight during the day, but she refused to let those battles steal their nights too. Nothing, she vowed, was going to darken the beauty she and Justin had found together in each other's arms.

"Trust me to know my limits. I promise you I won't push past them."

He gazed into her eyes for several long moments. Weighing. Assessing. Fighting with himself—with his desires *and* his worries. Finally, he nodded. "Wherever you take me, I'll follow."

She wanted to grab, to devour, to greedily gobble him up. But she needed him to trust her, to truly believe that she wouldn't put herself in harm's way during their lovemaking.

Still, just because she was going to go slow, didn't mean she wanted him to keep his clothes on. Last night, she'd let him strip her while he remained clothed. Tonight, things were going to go in the opposite direction.

With his zipper already down, she needed only to give his jeans a tug for them to fall. His boxers went too, which meant that his gorgeous, tanned, muscular body was now fully at her disposal.

Joy—and a huge rush of sensual anticipation—bubbled up inside of her as she ran her hands over his chest. Muscles and tendons jumped beneath her fingertips, prompting her to press kisses all over his delicious skin. "You're the yummiest thing I've ever tasted." She couldn't wait to take another taste, this time with her tongue in all the places she'd kissed.

His hands, which had slid into her hair, tightened. Though he was still gentle, she liked feeling his control slipping. Little by little, she intended to keep drawing away his self-control until he forgot everything but desire.

Moving slowly enough that he'd have no reason for alarm, she went to her knees in front of him, letting her nails drag lightly over his skin as she made her way down his body.

Oh my. He was beautiful.

Beyond beautiful.

Pleasure hummed in her throat as her lips made contact with his hot skin. And when her tongue shot out of its own volition to run a wet path up his flesh, he was so wonderfully, deliciously hard that her hum of pleasure turned into a full-on moan.

"Taylor." His fingers gripped her even more tightly as he tried to hold on to his control. But she could feel his hips wanting to move. Knew how badly he wanted to take what she so desperately wanted to give.

As far as she was concerned, there was no choice to make. She needed him—*all* of him—and wouldn't accept anything less.

His groans of pleasure reverberated through her small cottage. It was her favorite sound *ever*, one she'd never get tired of hearing. Heat coursed through her veins, pulsing hottest at her breasts and between her thighs. She wanted to rub herself all over him, wanted to drive herself high and then tease them both by lingering at the edge before they tumbled over together.

But first, she wanted Justin to let himself be wholly lost in her, the way she was utterly lost in him.

Wrapping one hand around the base of his shaft, she reached up to thread the fingers of her free hand with his. Her intimate kisses were no longer soft now, her pace no longer slow. Not when she could feel him pulsing with need and knew how close he was to ecstasy.

There were so many things she wanted, but none more in that moment than being the one to take him so high that he forgot about ever coming down.

And as she poured every ounce of her love into him, he finally let himself go, with her name falling from his lips again and again, as he told her how beautiful, how perfect she was, how much he loved her, that he'd never stop loving her.

Just the way she'd never stop loving him.

★ ★ ★

This was heaven. It had to be.

After Taylor had rocked his world to the core, Justin carried her into her bedroom and stripped her bare.

She'd just driven him over the edge with her mouth, and he should be sated, but he wasn't. Not even close. Fortunately, given the way she pushed him back onto the bed and prowled up his body, her hands, her mouth roaming with abandon over him, she was nowhere near sated either.

And yet, at the same time, he was terrified that he'd forget to be careful with her, that the force of his desire would accidentally hurt her.

"I love you." She straddled him as she spoke, her hips restlessly moving over his, making him ache with wanting her again mere minutes after release. She took his face in her hands. "I've always loved you."

For so many years, he'd loved her from afar, even when he was sitting right next to her, because he thought she loved her boyfriend. At long last, he knew that just because she'd been physically faithful to her ex, that didn't mean her heart hadn't been Justin's all along.

"From the first moment we met," he told her as he stroked her bare curves, "I wanted you. Craved you. Loved you." He wanted her to understand that no one else had ever touched his heart. "Only you." Regret over their lost years seized him again. "I should have fought for you. I shouldn't have stood on the sidelines and let you be with anyone else."

"Can't you see?" Her voice was gentle. Passionate.

"That's one of the reasons I love you. Because you let me make mistakes. You let me go down the wrong path—lots of wrong paths—and then figure out for myself what the right path might be. Everyone else in my life has always kept me inside a safe little box, but you never have." She brought her hands over his at her hips and threaded their fingers together. "Even now, you're trusting me to know my own limits, instead of telling me what my limitations are."

He understood why her family wanted to protect her, why they would never want any harm to come to their bright and utterly beautiful daughter, especially after losing a child. When they added in her diagnosis, that urge to insulate, to shelter, would be nearly irrepressible.

But no one thrived inside a cage, even one built with the best intentions. He couldn't do that to her, couldn't say he was only looking out for her while locking her up in a bubble where nothing could ever touch her. So he needed to start now, by trusting her to know her own body, her passion, her physical limits. He couldn't make those decisions for her by holding back.

Tugging her hands, he pulled her up his body, swiftly enough that he heard air rush from her lungs. "Justin?" Her hips were over his chest now, and she was looking down at him with an expression of surprise...and what looked like heady anticipation.

"A little higher," he said. "That's where I need you." He scooted down the bed beneath her, and then he did what he knew they both wanted: He lifted his mouth to her core, covering her hot, slick flesh and letting himself take a long, delicious taste of her.

Her hands tightened over his. *"Justin."* His name was a moan instead of a question this time as he used their linked hands on her hips to rock her over his mouth as he alternately teased her arousal with the tip of his tongue, then went deep. Again and again, he brought her to the edge, then forced himself to slow down and draw out her pleasure.

He could have played like that all night, her spicy-sweet taste on his tongue, her lithe body molten over him, but soon, she was dictating the pace, her gasps coming faster and faster until she finally broke apart in a trembling climax.

Rational thought was nearly out of reach when he slid her back down his body a short while later. All he knew was that he needed to be inside of her more than he needed to breathe. Only at the last second did he remember protection, and thank God, tonight the little packet was waiting in the night table beside the bed.

Moments later, Taylor was lowering herself onto him. If he'd been in heaven earlier, now he was in a nirvana that only one woman on earth could show him.

Together, they moved in a fluid dance of love and mind-blowing pleasure. Her eyes were closed, her head flung back as she used his hands, his arms, for leverage while she rode him with sweet abandon, chasing her pleasure, and his too.

He'd never seen anything so breathtaking in his entire life as Taylor giving herself to him, and when she finally crested her second peak, he had to kiss her as her release spun out into his.

For long moments afterward, they lay panting in each other's arms. She was sprawled over him, and he'd never felt so content. So happy. Or so amazed.

His soft laughter had her lifting her head from his chest. "Let me in on the joke."

"No joke," he said as he kissed her again. "It's just that I can hardly believe so many of the fantasies I've had about you are actually coming true."

She raised an eyebrow. "How many fantasies have you had about me?"

"Hundreds." No, that wasn't even close. "Thousands." Even that wasn't true. "Millions."

She laughed, a sound that covered him with as much warmth as her body over his. "Promise me you'll tell me all of them. Promise me we'll *do* all of them."

"Starting tonight?"

She gave him a naughty little smile that got his motor revving again in an instant. "We've wasted enough time, don't you think?"

"Not anymore," he said, then began to kiss every beautiful inch of her, the way he'd always longed to in his fantasies.

Only to find out that the reality was so much better.

CHAPTER TWELVE

Last night had been pure fantasy. This morning felt closer to a nightmare.

So far today, they'd both had a dozen vials of blood drawn at the UC Davis transplant center, and then Justin had been taken into his donor-evaluation meetings. But before he left, he'd given Taylor a kiss so hot it was clearly meant to wipe her mind clean of everything except memories of their breathless lovemaking.

But though her body heated up all over, she couldn't shake her rampantly conflicted thoughts about Justin offering to donate a kidney to her.

Too antsy to sit still on one of the padded blue chairs in the waiting room, she headed outside into the sunny, slightly crisp air. The weather had only recently started to turn cooler, but thankfully, Justin had grabbed her coat when they'd left this morning. Nervous about their visit to the transplant center, she'd gotten ready on autopilot—she could barely remember taking a shower and getting dressed. Even seeing

Justin's sister Maddie again after so many years had hardly registered. Under any other circumstances, Taylor would have wanted a big catch-up. Thankfully, Maddie had seemed to understand, giving Taylor a warm hug and saying, "Don't worry about a thing, I've got your B&B covered for as long as you need me." The next thing Taylor knew, she was in the passenger seat of Justin's rental car and they were on their way to Davis.

During the hour-long drive, he'd told her stories about his childhood, about scrapes he and his siblings had gotten into, about adventures they'd had together. She'd laughed in the right places, but she hadn't really been present, something he must have been aware of. It was, she assumed, why he'd kept up a running one-sided conversation—so that she would only be able to freak out with half a brain, rather than letting nerves take her over completely.

The sun warmed her while she walked through campus, and she unzipped her coat halfway. She'd been to UC Davis before—she'd met with doctors all over the Bay Area since her diagnosis—but she'd never been in any state of mind to appreciate how lovely the campus was. Looking up at the thick canopy of walnut branches, she forced herself to stop, to breathe, to notice the way the leaves were just starting to turn color, the green threaded with faint hints of red and orange and yellow.

Soon, the trees would be vibrant with fall color. She'd always loved autumn in California, the way the sky was almost always clear, which meant you could still hike and bike and have picnics outside, but then in the evening when the temperature dropped, you could light a fire and sit, warm and toasty, beside it with a mug of hot chocolate.

As she walked, she realized that somewhere along the way in these past few months, she had started to dread the coming of fall. She'd started to hate the passage of time, simply because she was afraid that time was the very last thing she had.

She'd always tried to be hopeful. Even when it had felt as though she was living a life that someone else had scripted, even after Justin had left for Germany, she'd never wanted to pull the covers over her head and not get up. She couldn't let herself fall to pieces now, not when she finally had the kind of love she'd never dared believe could be hers.

Just days ago, she'd told Justin how working on renovating her grandfather's home and turning it into a B&B had shown her that as long as she didn't give up, she could do anything she set her mind to. He'd seemed surprised that she hadn't already known that about herself, had acted as though she'd been foolish not to give herself credit for being strong.

This morning, she needed to hold on to that belief. Needed to hold on to her determination to never give up, never stop fighting for a long and healthy life!

Turning back, she headed toward the hospital, so she'd be waiting for Justin with a smile, with a hug, with a kiss when he emerged from his evaluation meetings. Yes, she was still deeply conflicted about him being her donor, but since they didn't even know yet if he would be a match, she wouldn't let herself borrow trouble.

One day at a time. That was how she needed to take things. And she was going to do her darnedest to appreciate each and every day that came, without letting herself sink into the trap of dreading potential problems that might, or might not, come.

She was about to step inside the hospital's double doors when her phone buzzed with her mother's ring tone. Knowing better than to ignore her mom's calls two days in a row, she picked up.

"I had a dream that you were in the hospital," her mother said with no preamble. "Please tell me it's just my mind playing tricks on me."

Wow, talk about mother's intuition. Taylor had never lied to her mom before, but over the past few months, she'd learned that oversharing wasn't a great idea either. She didn't want to keep her in the dark, but at the same time, it often seemed better to carefully and slowly dole out test results and prognoses. She could only imagine how distressed she'd be if she were in her mother's position.

"I'm actually at UC Davis right now—"

"Oh God, what's happened?"

"I just needed to get some blood work done."

She couldn't say that she was there because Justin wanted to donate a kidney to her. Regardless of the way her mother felt about him, Caroline would have no compunction about Taylor accepting his kidney. First and foremost, Taylor didn't want to get her mother's hopes up that Justin would be a match, when the odds were long against it. And if he *did* end up being compatible with her—her mom would probably hold him hostage until he was under the knife.

Still, Taylor knew better than to keep news of Justin's arrival in St. Helena to herself for any longer than she already had. It would only end up looking suspicious, as though she had something to hide. She'd already hidden her feelings for him for too many years. She couldn't stand the thought of hiding them another second.

"I'm not here alone," she said. "Justin is with me. He's actually staying in St. Helena this week, at my B&B."

"*Justin Morrison* is staying at your bed-and-breakfast?" Her mother sounded stunned. "I thought he was in Germany." Where Caroline had clearly hoped he'd stay forever, five thousand miles away from her daughter.

"He's in town for his brother's wedding this coming weekend," Taylor explained. But before she could say how wonderful it was to see him again—and that they weren't just friends anymore—her mother cut in.

"I thought you'd barely heard from him."

"That wasn't his fault, Mom, it was both of us. But we've talked everything through, and we're good again. Better than good, actually." Reminding herself that she was twenty-seven, not seventeen, she barreled on before her mother could interrupt again. "We're together now. As a couple."

"Together? A couple?" Horror rang out in her mother's voice. "Have you forgotten what he was like in college?"

"Of course not. He was my best friend."

"Who toyed with countless girls," her mother countered. "But even more than that, he loved stringing you along."

"That's not fair," Taylor protested. "Not any of it." Okay, so Justin had never lacked for female company. And she couldn't keep her gut from twisting when she thought about all the years she'd watched him go out with other people, even though she'd had a boyfriend the whole time.

Love, it turned out, wasn't always rational. Which was a large part of the reason she knew her mother didn't mean to hurt her. It was simply that love—and remembered loss—made her mother hold on a little too tightly sometimes.

Taylor suddenly found herself thinking about what Justin had said in the garden, how his mom was always after them to speak up, even if they were scared. If only Taylor could talk to her mother about the sister she'd never known—maybe then she could find a way to reassure her that Taylor would do everything in her power to ensure she wouldn't lose her too.

"He's why you broke up with Bruce, isn't he?" Caroline's voice broke into her thoughts. "Not because you wanted to start fresh in Napa with a new house and career, but because you could never get over your crush on him!"

"I broke up with Bruce because we never should have been together in the first place." Taylor was trying to remain calm, but it hurt to have these accusations thrown at her. Especially when there was at least a tiny thread of truth to them. Particularly the part where she'd never gotten over her college crush on Justin.

"You and Bruce were perfect together," her mother insisted. "Just *perfect!*"

"No, we weren't. We were settled and boring." She

hated to hurt her mom in any way, but Taylor refused to feel guilty, and wouldn't apologize, for wanting *breathless* and *sexy* and *exciting*. Especially now, when it would be all too easy to see nothing but struggles ahead if she wasn't so damned determined to hold on to hope and appreciate the beauty around her. "I'm in love with Justin. And he's in love with me."

Her mother was silent for a moment, obviously regrouping after her initial panicked responses. "Taylor, please," she cajoled, "you have to see this isn't what you need right now. That *he* isn't what you need. More than ever, you need to have a stable life. Your new business is already enough stress on your plate— you need to be surrounded by people who love you, who have always loved you, who will take care of you no matter what. You need someone you can trust at your side, not someone who comes and goes when it suits him."

Taylor tried to be understanding—this wasn't just about her, it was also about the daughter her parents had lost so many years ago. Her mother would do anything to keep Taylor and her brother safe.

"You don't have to worry about Justin hurting me," she said in a voice that she hoped came across as gentle but also firm. "I promise you that he would never hurt me in a million years." It was exactly the opposite, in fact—Justin had made it abundantly clear that he'd choose hurting himself over hurting her.

Just then, he walked out of the transplant center. He looked confident and handsome. Every eye turned to watch him as he covered the distance between them.

A shiver went through Taylor as she realized that he was hers now.

"I have to go now, Mom. I'll give you a call tomorrow. And don't worry," she added, making sure to say the mantra she ended every call with. "Everything's going to be okay."

She barely had time to shove the phone back into her pocket before Justin pulled her into his arms and kissed her.

"Damn, you taste good," he said against her lips. "I don't think I'll ever be able to get enough of you."

Despite her nerves having returned with a vengeance during her mom's call, she couldn't help but say in a breathless voice, "I won't ever be able to get enough of you either."

He nuzzled her neck, making every last part of her melt against him. But though it would be easier just to focus on how much they wanted each other, there was no point in hiding from reality.

"How was your meeting?" she asked.

He didn't lift his mouth from where he was nibbling at her earlobe. "Great."

She wanted to beg him to take her somewhere private where they could finish what he was starting. Instead, she forced herself to say, "What kind of information did they ask for during the evaluation?"

With obvious reluctance, he drew back. "I met my independent donor advocate, and we talked through my physical, mental, and emotional well-being."

"Did you tell your advocate that we're together?"

"I sure as hell did. I told her I love you, that I've always loved you, and that I would do anything for you."

It was one thing to hear him say those words to her and only her, but to know that he'd said them to a stranger was overwhelming. "Did you also tell her—" God, she hated to ask this, but she had to know just how forthright he'd been with the counselor who would be instrumental in helping him decide whether to actually go through with donating a kidney if they were a match. "About your mother?"

"I did." Grief flashed in his eyes for a split second before he said, "I told her I would have done anything to save my mom and that I've been working like hell for the past five years to come up with a cure."

"Did she think that maybe there was some kind of…transference going on? With me?" She fumbled for the right words, not at all convinced that she had them. "That maybe because you couldn't save your mom then, you'll do anything to save me now, even if it means putting yourself in danger?"

"Taylor." He stroked her cheek with the back of his hand. "I'll never stop missing my mom, but even if I had been able to save her, I would still want to do this for you. *With* you. Which is why I passed the evaluation with flying colors—and the physical they gave me too. We've already moved on to the informed-consent part."

She knew what informed consent was all about, where they made sure donors fully understood the risks and benefits of being a donor, how it could affect their lives both now and in the future, and that they could delay or stop the process at any time, even on the day of surgery, if need be.

"The good news," he continued, "is that there happens to be a donor in Yountville who said she'd be happy to tell her story and answer any questions I've got. Instead of just talking on the phone, I'm going to head over to her house to talk in person. It would be good if you came too."

"I don't know." She really didn't, could barely tell which way was up anymore. "Maybe it would be best if you went by yourself."

"I know you're still trying to wrap your head around everything," he said in a gentle voice, "but surely meeting a past donor in person and seeing how well she's doing—and how happy she is with her decision to donate—will go a long way to helping you let go of some of your concerns."

Feeling even more like she was on a runaway train than she had since getting her diagnosis, she said in a slightly desperate tone, "We don't even know if you're going to be a match yet." She was trying not to borrow trouble, but it was so hard...

"I've got this feeling in my gut." He took her hands and laid them on his chest so that she could feel the beating of his heart. "And here too. I know we're going to be a match. And when it turns out that I am, my advocate is confident she can fast-track everything. Instead of the process taking up to six months, she's going to pull out all the stops to get the transplant scheduled ASAP. The only possible holdup would be the final approval from the Human Tissue Authority, which could take a couple of weeks. But as soon as we have that, we'll be good to go."

All her life, Taylor had been swept along by other people's plans. By their decisions. She couldn't let that happen again. Especially now, when it wasn't just her health, her life, her future at stake.

"Justin, please, you need to slow down."

"And just stand by twiddling my thumbs while you get sicker? No way." He was as passionate as she had ever seen him. "You know as well as I do that the sooner I get all the tests done and confirm my compatibility for the transplant, the sooner you'll be better."

She couldn't argue with that, but she could point out a different truth. "You didn't come home to spend all your time and energy on lining up doctors and tests. You were supposed to have this week off from stress, from labs and hospitals, so that you could spend time with your family and enjoy your brother's wedding. You only have a few more days before you head back to Germany. You should make the most of them with the people you love."

He tugged her even closer then, as though he didn't want anything at all keeping them apart. "That's exactly what I'm doing—I'm spending my time with the person I love most of all. *You*. And I'm not going back to Germany. I'm due a break anyway, and like I said yesterday, I can set up a lab here."

There was nothing she wanted more than for him to stay here with her. But she couldn't be selfish. "It will take time to set up a new lab and to find scientists you want to work with. Your research is too important to be stalled like that." Frustration bubbled up and over. "This is one of the biggest reasons why I didn't tell you about my diagnosis! Because you have a life. An important one that you can't give up for me."

"Once you're better, I can turn my attention back to finding a cure for breast cancer. But the fact is that my mother is gone and no amount of research will ever bring her back." He was as fierce and as frustrated now as she was. "She's gone, Taylor, but you're still here. And I'm damn well going to do whatever it takes to make sure you stay that way."

She tried to hold back her tears, but with Justin's arms around her, she couldn't stop the breakdown. And she knew why—she felt safe with him. Safer than she'd ever felt with anyone else. Safe enough to stop trying to hold herself together every single second and give in to a few seconds of feeling shattered and scared.

"I wish I just felt one thing, one way, instead of shifting all over the place from second to second," she said, her words slightly muffled against his chest. "I'm happy. I'm scared. I'm hopeful. I'm guilty." She lifted her face to look at the man who was her best friend *and* her lover. "I'm desperate for a donor, but I'm also desperate for that donor not to be you." She wanted to scream in frustration. "Now that we've found each other again, now that we're finally together, why can't everything be easier? Why can't we have just a little bit of happiness without all of this?"

★ ★ ★

Justin hated to see Taylor cry, even though he knew bottling up her tears would only make her feel worse. Thank God he was here to stroke her hair, to wipe the tears away, to hold her, and to make sure she knew that he was always going to be here for her, no matter what.

When he'd left the hospital just minutes ago, he'd been so sure, so certain that everything would be okay. He'd felt so positive. But he'd stupidly forgotten that he wasn't the only one who needed to make decisions about their future.

Whether she realized it or not, Taylor had always been her own woman, with a strong mind and purpose and sense of right. Sure, he could dig out every trick in the book to try to persuade her to do things his way—and, honestly, at this point, he wasn't ruling anything out. Not when her health was on the line. But deep in his heart, he knew better.

He knew the right choice for him. But Taylor needed to make her own decision about what was right for *her*.

"I've gotten your shirt all wet," she said as she wiped away the rest of her tears with the back of her hand. Taking a deep breath, she said, "How about we grab a cup of coffee at the Student Union before we head back?"

There was so much more he wanted to say to her, a dozen additional arguments he had ready to get her to see things his way. But she'd already told him to slow down, and he needed to heed her warning, or risk pushing her away.

The thought of losing Taylor's love gutted him, down to the marrow.

Not yet trusting himself to say anything that wouldn't put her on the defensive, he simply held her hand as they headed over to the campus café. While they walked in silence, he remembered what the transplant coordinator had told him—that hope, fear, sorrow, and love were at the heart of nearly every organ transplant. The woman had explained how hard this decision could be for people in Taylor's position, and how Taylor's biggest fear was likely that he would be harmed during or even recovery.

He'd listened carefully—at least, he thought he had. But the truth was that when he'd come back outside to Taylor, he'd still been barreling through her life, and her choices, like that bull in the china shop.

As they ordered then waited for their coffees, he made a silent vow to be more understanding of where she was coming from, even if it wouldn't change his decision about wanting to be her donor. He'd always respected Taylor's opinions and her beliefs. He couldn't use loving her and wanting to help her as an excuse to act differently now.

She was desperate for some simple happiness. He racked his brain to think of something fun they could do to give them a few hours of respite. No question about it, they needed something to make them laugh and take the pressure off for a little while. Thankfully, that was when his eye caught on a flyer stapled to the announcement board on the opposite wall for the St. Helena Grape Stomp Competition.

He sent a quick text to his sister, then turned to Taylor once he had Maddie's reply. "What do you say we do a little grape stomping?"

Clearly lost in her thoughts, Taylor looked at him in confusion. "Grape stomping?"

"Yup." He grinned at her, pointing at the flyer. "There's a competition in your town this afternoon that's got our names all over it."

"It sounds fun, but I don't want to take advantage of Maddie's generosity."

"She's happy to cover for as long as we need her." He held up his phone so Taylor could see his sister's reply to his text asking if she could stay a few hours longer. "It's right here, in her own words—she's having a fabulous time and baking in your kitchen is just what she needed after a crazy week working in the city."

Seeing the spark in Taylor's eyes, the one that told him she wanted to go stomp some grapes even if she thought she should go back and relieve Maddie of her kitchen duties, he decided now was one of those times when it was good to be a bit of a china-smashing bull. "It won't take long—and then once we've won the big prize, we'll head straight back to your B&B."

"My mother always did think you were a bad influ-ence," she said, but she was smiling as she said it. A smile full of enough relief that he knew a break from the stress of any further tests or big decisions for an afternoon was exactly the right thing.

Hopefully, everything else would become equally clear very, very soon.

CHAPTER THIRTEEN

Taylor couldn't believe they were about to stomp grapes. Only Justin could have gotten her out here, with her jeans rolled up to her knees and her feet bare.

They were standing together, her back to his front, his arms wrapped around her waist, as they waited their turn. Ten teams had signed up for the competition. Although there would be several small prizes given out to the groups that squeezed the most juice out of the grapes with their feet, it was obvious that this wasn't really a competition, but rather a chance for the community to come together to celebrate the vineyards and the wines for which St. Helena was world famous. Several people Taylor had met during the past months had already come by to say hello.

Today, she didn't hesitate to let everyone know that Justin was her boyfriend. And not just because he'd told her that he was planning to set up a lab nearby so that he could stay with her in St. Helena. The miles between California and Germany had never truly been the issue. They could have weathered that if they had to. Perhaps someone on the outside looking in would think that their relationship had moved really fast in the past forty-eight hours—from making love to declaring their feelings to making big career and location changes. But they'd had eight years to build to where they were now.

Eight years of longing. Eight years of secret loving.

She might be confused and conflicted about plenty of other things in her life, but her feelings for Justin were perfectly, beautifully clear.

Laughter and hilarity rang out while the first couple made an absolute mess of their barrel of grapes. Resting her head against Justin's chest, she let herself relax for the first time all day. The song "Stomp Them Grapes" was playing on repeat, while a couple of large-screen TVs had been set up showing the *I Love Lucy* episode where Lucille Ball made stomping grapes look like the funniest thing in the world.

Taylor laughed as she watched Lucille Ball go totally crazy in the grape vat—one of the teams competing was actually dressed up as Lucy and the grape stomper—and it felt good to feel "normal" for a little while. The morning's coolness had given way to a wonderfully warm afternoon, and Taylor loved being able to bask in the sun as she closed her eyes and turned her face toward the sky.

It would be all too easy to let herself dwell on bad lab reports and blood work, to forget about fun while she spent all of her time weighing difficult decisions. Justin was right. Not only did they need a break from the heaviness of it all, but being here today as a part of her new community served as yet another reminder about the good decisions she had already made to quit her office job in Palo Alto and move to St. Helena.

"They've just called our team name," Justin said, his breath at her ear sending a delicious shiver through her despite the warmth of the sun. "Are you ready for Team Super Stomp to dominate?"

She spun into his arms, laughing at the team name he'd come up with as she kissed him. "I love you." She never wanted him to forget it, didn't want him to think that her reticence to accept his offer to be her donor meant she didn't care for him more deeply than she did anyone else. "No matter what."

He gazed into her eyes, making her feel as though they were the only people for miles, even in the middle of a big crowd. "No matter what."

Hand in hand, they walked over to their barrel, which had already been loaded up with dark purple grapes. "Your goal today," the volunteer in charge reminded them, "is to extract the most juice out of measured amounts of wine grapes. I'm assuming you will be the stomper?" he said to Taylor, making his guess based on her rolled-up jeans and bare feet. "Please step into the foot wash." Turning to Justin, he said, "Your job as the swabber will be to stand outside the barrel and catch the juice in this bucket. Don't hesitate to reach inside the barrel to assist your stomper to ensure a free flow of juice through the screen and out the drain spout. Got it?"

Justin nodded, the beauty of his grin making Taylor's heart flip inside her chest.

She'd been a fool not to tell him about her diagnosis months ago when she'd first found out. And she'd been an even bigger fool to let their friendship slide away after he left Stanford for Germany. She'd never make a mistake like that again. No matter what happened from here on out, she would never take Justin's friendship, or his love, for granted again.

What they had, she now understood, was the most rare and precious thing in the world. Something to fight for, against all odds.

"Stomper," the volunteer said to her, "please take your position inside the barrel."

Justin held on to her hands as she carefully made her way up the stairs and onto the mound of grapes. "It feels so weird," she said, wrinkling her nose at the strange feel of the fruit already popping apart beneath her feet. She took a step and realized how slippery it was.

"Your hands go here." Justin placed them on the side rim of the barrel so that she was leaning over slightly at the waist in his direction. "As long as you keep holding on, you should be steady. But don't worry, I won't let you fall."

"I know you won't," she said, then bent down a little farther so that they could kiss.

The volunteer held up a stopwatch. "Five-second countdown. Five, four, three, two, *start stomping!*"

Justin's kiss had sent so much happiness shooting through her, that the second she was let loose in the barrel, she became a wild stomping machine. Grape skins and dark purple juice flew in every direction, most of it up onto her jeans and T-shirt and the bare skin of her arms, legs, and face—but also onto Justin, who wasn't at all spared by standing outside the barrel, holding the bucket under the drain spout and cheering her on.

"No one can stomp grapes the way you can, Taylor!" he yelled. "You're amazing! You're unstoppable! You're a Super Stomper!"

Though she was majorly out of breath, she couldn't stop laughing. Stomping grapes was one of the grossest—and most fun—things she had done in a very long time. Grape juice was flowing from the barrel into Justin's bucket with such speed that he barely had time to put it down and pick up another one before it overflowed. The crowd had gathered around them, and soon, Justin was leading the group in a rousing chorus of "Super Stompers! Super Stompers! Super Stompers!"

She had nearly run out of steam when the stop-watch dinged again. Still laughing, Justin pulled her out of the barrel and swung her around. He kissed her until she was even more breathless, and when he finally let her go, she stumbled slightly, directly into the path of their two full buckets of grape juice.

Both buckets knocked into one another, then bumped out in the opposite direction, toppling over before anyone could stop them.

"Oh no." She looked at Justin with wide eyes. "I actually thought we might have a chance of winning."

"It's okay." He hugged her tighter. "We've already won the biggest prize of all, don't you think?"

He was right. Even when they'd been only friends back in college, she'd already felt like she'd won the lottery. Who else had a best friend so smart and funny and sweet and caring? And now, with love on their side, surely they could triumph over even the most difficult problems. Couldn't they?

"Thank you for bringing me here today." She held his face in her hands, even more mesmerized by him than she had been the first time she'd set eyes on him. "It was exactly what I needed." Her side was aching a little bit after all the exertion, but it was nothing compared to the pain she'd felt when she collapsed on the stairs. *"You're* exactly what I need."

No question about it—she had already won the biggest prize of all.

★ ★ ★

"I had the *best* time today!" Maddie greeted them at the door with a tray of brownies that smelled so good Taylor's mouth instantly began to water. She'd never been a huge one for sweets, but she couldn't resist taking a brownie as she said profuse thanks to Justin's sister for stepping in to run her B&B while they were out. Still warm from the oven, the brownie melted on her tongue.

"You're a magician in the kitchen," Taylor said to Maddie. Moaned it, actually. "I've been making cookies—"

"Great cookies," Justin chimed in.

"—but my baked goods are nothing compared to this." An idea came to her. "I know how busy you are already, but if there was any chance that you would consider baking for me every now and again, that would be amazing."

"I'd love to!" Maddie looked even happier now. "How much would you need? How often? And would you just want brownies or cookies and scones and cakes? I could make madeleines and macarons, if you want more of a French flavor."

"I want all of it," Taylor said, loving Maddie's enthusiasm. "How about once a week to start? Then more if I manage to get my idea for an afternoon tea off the ground in a few months." She was still on too much of a high from their grape-stomping adventure to let in dark thoughts about what her health might be like in a few months—and what impact that might have on her business. "And I'll bet once some of the locals taste your treats, the stores around here will want some too."

"Why did you ever leave her and go to Germany?" Maddie asked Justin, with an elbow to his gut.

"Because I was an idiot," he said.

"We both were." Taylor put her hand into Justin's in case his sister didn't already know that they were together now.

Of course, word traveled fast in the Morrison family, and Maddie's eyes were twinkling as she said, "Drew told me the good news. You two are perfect together. I'm so happy for you."

"Thanks, I'm really happy too." Taylor knew she was beaming, especially when Justin gave her a kiss in front of his sister. "If you two don't mind holding the fort for a few more minutes, I'll go wash off and get changed."

She was pretty sure the grape stains on her skin weren't going to scrub off completely any time soon, but that was okay. She liked looking down and remembering how fun it had been to stomp grapes with Justin today. For a little while at least, she'd felt free and normal, like there was nothing wrong with her whatsoever.

★ ★ ★

"Drew told me about Taylor's diagnosis," Maddie said once Taylor had gone out to her cottage. "I looked up some stuff online, but you know I've never had much of a science brain, so I was having a hard time wrapping my head around it. In plain English, how bad is it?"

Justin appreciated Maddie waiting to ask her questions until Taylor had left. It wasn't that he intended to keep this conversation from her—it was more that he didn't want anything to bring her down. It had been so good to see her laugh and relax and let go of her worries for a couple of hours. He still hoped that she would come with him to meet the local donor tomorrow and hear what the woman had to say, but until then, he planned to do whatever he could to keep Taylor's mind off it.

In clear and simple terms, he explained Taylor's diagnosis. Unfortunately, the more he told Maddie, the more his sister's face fell. "But she'll be okay, won't she? If you give her your kidney?"

"First, I have to be a match."

"You will be." Maddie looked just as determined as he felt.

"When I am," he said with a small smile, "kidney transplants can work really well."

"All the time?"

"Most of the time."

"And when a transplant doesn't work well?"

He shook his head, unable to let himself go there. He was a scientist, but that didn't mean he believed in trusting *only* lab results. He'd read enough studies over the years to understand that science alone couldn't account for one hundred percent of healing. Hope, faith, and love were also extremely important.

"I love her, Maddie. I'll do anything for her. I won't let anything happen to her."

His sister didn't ask any more questions, just put her arms around him and held on tight. It wasn't the first time they'd held each other this way—they'd needed each other just as much six years before, when their mother had gotten sick, then passed away.

"Make sure she knows we're all here for her, okay?"

For a few moments, he didn't think he could trust his voice. "Thanks again for stepping in today. You've already helped more than you know. Not just so that we could do the blood tests and meet with the doctors, but because she needed an afternoon in the sunshine most of all."

Maddie gripped his hands and squeezed them, before getting up. "I should probably go before Taylor comes back. Otherwise, I'll start crying and ruin the fun grape-stomping vibe you guys had going on." She went into the kitchen for her bag, then came out and gave Justin another hug. "Tell her to call me anytime. For any reason. And let her know that I love her. We all do."

After walking his sister out to her car, Justin went upstairs to change his grape-stained clothes before Taylor's guests came back from sightseeing and wine tasting to partake of afternoon tea and brownies.

By the time Taylor returned from her cottage and brought in the tea, the parlor was full of happy, slightly sunburned tourists—adults and children alike stuffing themselves full of Maddie's brownies. Taylor put her arm around him.

"You're a natural with my guests. Especially," she said as she looked down at his fresh pair of jeans, already smudged with chocolate from where he'd been playing Lego with the kids in the corner, "with the littlest ones."

Another vision hit him, clear and vibrant, of Taylor

pregnant and glowing with a child of their own. The first of many—he wanted their kids to grow up in the kind of loud, boisterous family that he'd so loved being a part of.

But he knew better than to say anything about his vision. Not because he was afraid she wouldn't feel the same way, but because he didn't want his dreams for their future to send her spiraling into worries about whether they could ever come to pass.

He knew they would.

Faith, hope, love—he would hold on to those, and to her, no matter what.

* * *

The Belmonts invited Taylor and Justin to dinner for their last evening in town, and they had a great meal at a Thai restaurant just up the valley in Calistoga. He loved having her all to himself, but he also loved watching her captivate everyone around her the way she'd always captivated him.

After they returned and said good night to her guests, they walked back through the moonlight to her cottage, arm in arm.

"I know it's really hard to pull up roots and put them somewhere new," she said, "but I really hope Katie and Brent and their kids end up deciding to move here."

"I'd be pretty surprised if they don't." Though he'd been with Taylor in St. Helena for only three nights, it already felt like coming home. He could have lived happily with her anywhere—in a desert or a jungle or smack-dab in the middle of suburbia—but there was something special about Napa Valley. Not only because of its picturesque vineyards and wineries, but also because after only a few days, he had seen firsthand how supportive and welcoming the community was. St. Helena was the perfect town to raise a family in, to watch kids' soccer games on weekend mornings, then play in the pool all afternoon. "This place is pretty hard to resist."

"Are you sure?" She stopped just inside her front door to face him. "Are you really ready to give up your life in Frankfurt and move here? I would never expect you to do that, especially this quickly. No one would."

"I've never been more sure." But this wasn't just about him, so he had to ask, even if the answer might not be the one he wanted to hear. "What about you? Earlier today, you said I was moving too fast." He stroked her cheek, needing to touch her. "Do you want me to move here? Do you want me with you? Or do you need some space, some time?"

"Of course I want you here with me," she said, sending a massive rush of relief coursing through him. "But what if you resent me one day for asking you to drop everything in your life and turn on a dime?"

"The only thing I'd resent is getting on an airplane on Monday to fly five thousand miles from the woman I love. I don't want to tell you *I love you* over Skype. I want to hold you in my arms when I say it." He was glad to see a small smile appear on her lips as he lowered his mouth to hers. When he was barely a breath away, he said, "I love you."

Their kiss was full of passion—and so much love it humbled him.

"You haven't gotten the grape juice off," she said as she ran her tongue over his collarbone. "Why don't I help you with that?"

Without waiting for his reply, she began stripping away his clothes, pulling his T-shirt over his head, then unzipping and shoving his jeans to the floor. Utterly mesmerized by her, before he knew it, she had her own clothes off and then was taking his hand in hers to lead him into the shower.

She turned the water on, then sat him down on the tiled seat at the far end. The warm spray rushed over her skin, rivulets of water streaming over her breasts and stomach as she picked up the soap and lathered up her hands.

Gently, with her palms moving across his skin, she ran soap bubbles over him. First over his face and neck, then down his shoulders and arms. Lifting his hands, she placed them on her stomach as she re-lathered with the soap, then worked on rubbing each finger with the bubbles, one at a time, to wash away the last traces of grape juice.

He loved the care she took with him. He could feel more than desire in her touch—he could feel her love for him in every stroke, every caress, as she made her way down his chest, his stomach muscles jumping beneath the light brush of her fingertips. By the time she started running her hands over his thighs, he didn't think he could handle much more. If she kept touching him like this, he was going to lose it long before he got a chance to reciprocate by lathering up her skin the same way.

"It's your turn now," he said, but when he got up to change places with her, she put her hand on his chest and gently pushed him back.

"It is my turn," she agreed, "but I don't need you to clean me up right now. I need you to *fill* me up."

He groaned at her deliciously filthy words as she reached for one of the condoms that they'd decided to keep stashed in the shower.

Slowly, perfectly, she lowered herself over him, and even as pleasure shot higher and higher, taking them both over the edge together, relief was there too.

Relief that after all these years, her heart was his—and his was hers.

Relief that she had allowed him to take her to the transplant center for the tests and was considering letting him help her.

Relief that she seemed so vibrant and healthy today, despite everything he'd read on her doctors' reports.

Making love with Taylor—and holding her close—was exactly what he needed tonight. All day he'd wanted to be strong for her. He'd wanted to make sure she laughed, rather than cried. He'd wanted her to focus on hopes rather than fears.

But the truth was that by this time of night, pretending he wasn't scared took a hell of a toll on him.

Burying his face against her chest, he let water from the shower cover the tears he suddenly couldn't hold back. And all the while, Taylor held him just as tightly.

Knowing it would be the very best way to build up their reserves of strength, after drying each other off with plush white towels, they slid together beneath the covers and kept on holding each other tight until morning.

CHAPTER FOURTEEN

As they headed through her garden the next morning, Taylor felt a million times better than she had twenty-four hours ago on their way to the transplant center. All because of Justin, who had made sure to keep them busy enough all afternoon that for once, while her worries still lingered in the background, they hadn't been front and center.

He was so good for her. She'd always known it, but in college, she had been too scared of rejection—and stepping outside of her comfort zone—to try for being more than just his friend. Even earlier this week, if he hadn't boldly taken her in his arms and tempted her to stop hiding from her desires, she likely would have wimped out.

Thankfully, as they walked up the back steps, then opened the kitchen door, she didn't need to worry about that anymore. All those wasted years with her ex were nothing more than a lukewarm memory.

At least, she'd thought the past was firmly in the

past...until she saw who was sitting in her kitchen drinking a cup of coffee.

"Bruce?" She blinked hard once, then again. Surely she couldn't be seeing what she thought she was seeing.

Her ex-boyfriend got up, his arms wide as though to hug her, then he stopped short as Justin came inside, the door slamming behind him.

"What are you doing here?" Justin's words were more growled than spoken.

Taylor had an instinctive urge to hold her arms out wide too, to block the two men from going after each other. Bruce had never been a particularly physical guy, but she'd never seen this kind of jealousy in his eyes either.

As for Justin, she could feel the heat of his fury behind her without turning to look.

"Your mother called me," Bruce said. "She told me what you've been going through. She said you needed me." He spoke as though Justin wasn't in the room, focusing only on her. "I took a red-eye to be here for you, baby."

"She isn't your *baby*." Justin sounded even less civil now, if that was possible. He took a step forward, but she put her hand on his chest.

"Justin." She had to say his name a second time to get him to look at her. "I'll deal with this."

She could see his indecision, knew he wanted to throw her ex out the door personally. But she also knew he trusted her not only to be able to deal with her ex, but also to know that she'd made the right choice in choosing him over Bruce.

At last, he said, "I'll be just outside if you need me."

"Thank you."

But he wouldn't let her go that fast, not without a kiss, one so possessive it should have made the feminist inside her protest. Instead, she went utterly weak in the knees, glad to be his, to know that he didn't just possess her, she possessed him too. In every way— mind, body, heart, soul.

He gave Bruce a look of warning as he passed him in the kitchen, one that promised swift and painful retribution if he hurt her in any way. She appreciated how badly Justin wanted to protect her, but she knew firsthand that Bruce was harmless.

"It's nice to see you," she said in as calm a voice as she could muster given what a huge and not particularly welcome surprise he was. "But I'm afraid I don't understand why you felt you needed to come all the way out here."

"I still love you, Taylor." Her eyes widened. It wasn't like Bruce to be so direct—he'd always tended to meander around whatever it was he was trying to say. "I had no idea you were facing such health struggles. To think that you might d—" His words crumbled in a choked-up throat.

"Everything is going to be okay," she said, rolling out her trusty mantra as she put her hand on his shoulder to guide him back to the stool. She was still irritated with him, but she couldn't help feeling sorry for him too. "I'll fill your cup and get you something to eat. That will make you feel better."

"You've got to give me another chance, baby."

Gritting her teeth at the fact that he obviously didn't know when to quit, she said, "Stop calling me *baby*."

"You always loved it when I called you that." He scowled over his shoulder at the direction in which Justin had gone. "Before *him*."

No, she hadn't loved it. Bruce calling her *baby* had made her feel like they were stuck in a fifties-era relationship where he was supposed to bring home the bacon and she was supposed to fry it up in a pan. After making sure the kids were bathed and in bed, of course, by the time he got home from his stressful job in a world far beyond her little homestead. It almost made her laugh as she realized that he did, in fact, have quite a high-powered job in banking, having risen quickly through the ranks in Rochester, and she was frying up quite a bit of bacon these days for her guests.

In any case, as she'd said to Justin a few days earlier, Bruce wasn't a bad guy. He just wasn't for her.

There was no point in hurting him further, so she didn't correct his erroneous assumption. She simply topped up his coffee and started scrambling eggs. She'd skip the bacon today.

"Your B&B is nice, Taylor."

She could see that he meant it, but his compliment didn't mean nearly as much to her as Justin's had when she'd given him the tour on his first day. Perhaps she should be gracious and offer Bruce a tour as well, but she wasn't feeling particularly gracious at the moment.

"Thank you." And then, since he'd made the effort of flying all the way out here, she asked, "How is everything going for you in Rochester? How's your job? Your family?" She made sure to look pointedly at him as she added, "Your girlfriend?" Her mother had slipped up on the phone a few weeks back and mentioned that he was dating someone. Taylor had been nothing but happy for Bruce. After all, he hadn't only wasted her years—she'd also wasted his.

"She's nothing to me. Not like you are."

Taylor fought the urge to roll her eyes. "Seriously, Bruce, you don't need to say that."

"You're the love of my life." He reached for her hand so that the spatula dropped onto the counter and she nearly burned herself on the iron skillet. "You're the light in my eyes. You're the beating of my heart!"

The kitchen door was flung open. Justin was obviously on high alert, and the sound of the stainless-steel spatula clanking onto tile had been enough to make him rush back in. Before she realized it, he had Bruce's shirt in his fists and was dragging him out of the kitchen.

"Justin," she said, "please, wait—"

The words dried up in her throat as another familiar face and figure came swinging in through the front door. Bruce wasn't the only one who had decided to surprise her with a visit.

Her mother had too.

* * *

Justin couldn't believe it. First, he and Taylor had to deal with her ex, who obviously wanted Taylor back. And now her mother, who hated Justin and wanted her to get back together with Bruce, was here too?

But when he caught sight of Taylor's face and saw how pale she was, he dropped her ex's shirt to rush over to help her to the couch, where he sat beside her and stroked her back until he felt her breathing return to normal.

She'd wanted to deal with Bruce on her own, and he knew how strong she was. But they were a team now, which meant they stood by each other, no matter what. And this kind of stress was the very last thing she needed right now.

"Oh, honey!" Her mother looked horribly upset as she sank to her knees in front of her daughter. "You swore you were taking care of yourself, but I can see that you aren't."

"She's been doing great until now," Justin told Taylor's mother before she could reply for herself.

Caroline Cardenes looked at him with barely concealed dislike. Actually, there was nothing concealed about it. "I'm Taylor's mother. I can see when my daughter is in pain." Dismissing him completely, she turned her entire focus on Taylor. "Sweetie, do you need to lie down? Or have something to drink? Or call the doctor?"

"Mom." Taylor held up a hand. "I'm fine. Everything's going to be okay."

Over the past few days, he had heard her say that enough times to realize it was a mantra of sorts. One he had the feeling she said more to soothe the people around her than because she actually believed it.

Footsteps sounded on the stairs. Taylor's guests were on their way down for one of her delicious breakfasts. Hearing it too, she stood. "I need to get to work."

"I'm here to take care of you now," her mother declared, "so you don't have to worry about anything anymore."

"If you'd like to help me make breakfast, that's fine, but I am going to do my job." Taylor's voice was low-pitched but full of steel. "And then when my guests are gone for the day, you and Bruce and I can have a chat."

Her mother looked stunned by her daughter's determination. "Of course, honey. I'll just go tidy up from my flight, and then you can let me know what you need help with in the kitchen."

Once her mother was gone, Taylor turned to Bruce. "I would appreciate it if you stayed right here until breakfast is ready." Her ex looked as though he might argue, but then nodded instead.

Justin was next in line. "We need to talk." Taking his hand, she pulled him out to the front porch. No doubt she was going to lay into him for manhandling her ex—but he'd do it again in a heartbeat. Even the guy putting his hand over hers was enough to make Justin see red. Bruce had touched her for the last time, as far as he was concerned.

"I love you," she said the moment the door closed behind them, "but I don't need you to fight my battles for me. Not with my mother or Bruce."

"I love you," he said back, "so I can't help but want to fight your battles." He was pleased when the corners of her mouth quirked up a tiny bit at his response, even if it hadn't been what she wanted to hear.

She sighed, finally letting her defenses down as she

said, "I can't believe they're here. I mean, it's always good to see my mom, but this drama with Bruce is just one more thing I don't want to deal with right now."

"However you need me, whatever you need me to do," he told her, "just say it, and I'll be there for you."

"Well, for starters, please try not to get into a fight with Bruce. I know the two of you aren't going to become friends." He couldn't hold back a snort at the thought of *ever* becoming friends with the guy. "But that doesn't mean you need to punch each other's lights out either." When his eyebrows went up, she said, "Okay, so I know the punching out would only go one way. But you know what I mean. And *second*, but even more important, you can't say anything to my mom about wanting to be a donor. She'll get her hopes up, and then if it doesn't work out, she'll be crushed."

"It's going to work out."

Taylor's eyes narrowed. "Just because you might be a compatible donor for me doesn't mean I'm going to let you do it."

Damn it, he knew better than to push her like this. But the shock of dealing with her surprise guests had made him forget he needed to go slowly, to make sure that any decisions were as much hers as his.

"You're right." He pulled her close and brushed a kiss on her forehead. "You don't need your mother breathing down your neck on top of everything else."

She rested her cheek against his chest for a moment, clearly relieved by his agreement. "I should go inside." She drew back with obvious reluctance. "Now remember, play nice with Bruce. Or, better yet," she said as she put her hand on the doorknob, "maybe you should go for a run and burn off some of that steam I can see coming out of your ears."

It was probably a good idea, but he didn't want to leave her alone with the guy. Who knew what Bruce would try to pull? Hell, Justin knew firsthand just how much it must hurt to have made the mistake of letting her go. There was nothing a guy wouldn't do to try to get her back, which was why Justin didn't trust Bruce as far as he could throw him.

Gritting his teeth, Justin had to deliberately relax his fists as he stepped inside. Bruce was standing by the window, acting like he was scrolling through messages on his phone, but Justin wouldn't be surprised if he'd had his face pressed up against the glass trying to read their lips while they'd been talking on the porch.

To be fair, her ex wasn't a bad-looking guy—tall and broad, with dark hair. Justin could see what Taylor must have found attractive about him all those years ago. But there was a weakness to his chin—and a smallness to his fingers—that tipped the scales in the wrong direction. To Taylor's mother, Bruce might seem like the safer choice, the choice she could not only predict but also dictate to, but he definitely wasn't the better choice. Not by a long shot.

"Your smile, and your huge heart, can charm absolutely anyone."

It was what Justin's mother used to say to him when he got bad-tempered over things not going his way. Everyone thought he was the more cerebral twin compared to Sean, but when push came to shove, Justin was actually the one more likely to push *and* shove. Probably because Sean had plenty of sports-based physical outlets for his frustration, whereas the lab wasn't exactly conducive to pitching a fit, unless Justin wanted to clean up shards of test tubes afterward.

Justin didn't care one whit about charming Bruce. Not bashing the guy's head in would be a win. But Caroline Cardenes was another matter entirely. Taylor loved her mother and respected her opinion. And one day soon, when Justin was more than just Taylor's boyfriend, he hoped to have Taylor's mother on *both* their sides.

The easiest way to get on her good side would be to tell her his plans to donate a kidney to her daughter. But he couldn't go back on his promise to keep that information between him and Taylor for now. So he'd have to do things the hard way—smiling when he felt like cursing and keeping his hands in his pockets when he felt like wringing Bruce's neck.

Justin had to prove to Taylor's mother that he was not only the better man for her daughter, but also someone she could count on to take care of Taylor the way she and her husband did. With pure, unconditional love.

Thankfully, he'd learned everything he needed to know about unconditional love from his parents. And as long as he kept his mother's voice in his head, he'd find a way to do what needed to be done.

Even when it meant walking up to Taylor's ex, holding out his hand, and saying, "Sorry about what happened earlier. I hope you'll agree to start over. I'm Justin Morrison, and it's nice to finally meet you after all these years."

CHAPTER FIFTEEN

As Caroline helped out in the kitchen and then with serving her guests, Taylor was glad she had the chance to see how well the B&B was running in its inaugural week. Even if Caroline's arrival had been a surprise, it wasn't an unwelcome one. Especially given that Taylor felt a little more tired than usual this morning. Her side wasn't hurting much, apart from that dull ache that she was pretty much used to by now. No doubt the shock of finding her ex sitting in her kitchen as she walked in with her new boyfriend had worn her down a bit.

A couple of hours later, everything in the kitchen and dining room was clean and put away. Rufus and Janet would be in soon to deal with the bathrooms, towels, and sheets. Confident that everything was in order, at least on the business front, Taylor brewed fresh coffee and plated the extra brownies that Maddie had stored in a glass container in the fridge.

As she walked into the parlor, she was pleased to see that Justin and Bruce seemed to have arrived at a truce. They were both on their computers—Justin likely doing more research on PKD—while her mother created a fresh flower display for the front window from the roses in Taylor's garden.

"I'd love it if the four of us could sit down and have a coffee break," Taylor said as she poured coffee into four mugs. She'd never been the kind to force an issue, or to ram an idea down someone's throat, but she didn't want there to be any misunderstanding from this point forward. Particularly when it came to Bruce.

A couple of minutes later, the four of them had each taken a mug and were sitting around the coffee table in the parlor.

"First of all," Taylor said, "I would like to rewind and start this morning again by saying how nice it is to see you, Mom, and you too, Bruce. Family and friends are always welcome here, and I hope you'll accept my invitation to stay in the two available rooms."

There wasn't so much as a flash of surprise on Justin's face. He would have done exactly the same thing for his own family. Putting herself in his shoes, however, she wouldn't have been at all happy to share the same space with one of his exes.

"Of course we'll stay, honey," her mother said. "That's a lovely offer, isn't it, Bruce?"

"It is," Bruce agreed, "but I've got to get back to the bank by tomorrow morning. I've just been alerted to a rather messy international transaction that one of my staff put through. Time, unfortunately, is of the essence."

"It certainly is," Taylor's mother said in a sharp voice, clearly displeased with him. "Which is why you should tell Taylor why you're here. Tell her your plans."

Taylor looked between the two of them. "Plans?"

When Bruce wasn't immediately forthcoming, her mother said, "Bruce wants to donate one of his kidneys to you."

Taylor's mouth dropped open as she spun to look at him. "That's why you came to St. Helena?"

He cleared his throat and pulled at his collar as though it were too tight, despite the fact that two buttons were already undone. "Well...after your mother told me about your diagnosis..." He looked like he'd rather be anywhere else, agreeing to anything else.

"Bruce." Taylor gave him a lopsided smile. "I appreciate your gesture. But you don't have to donate a kidney to me."

"I don't?"

"Of course he does, honey." Her mother's voice cracked with emotion. "If Bruce is a match, he's your very best option."

Taylor knew Justin had to be *dying* to speak up, but

he was keeping his promise. She'd told herself the reasons she'd given Justin to keep his donation offer quiet were perfectly rational, especially when it came to giving her mother false hope. But none of those were the real reasons.

Bluntly put, Taylor had asked him to remain silent because she was still afraid to live her own life and make her own decisions fully and completely. She was still afraid of making the wrong choices, still afraid of taking risks that might not always turn into rewards.

But she couldn't live like that anymore. If she wanted her parents to let go and see that she was a capable adult, perfectly well equipped to make even the hardest decisions, there was no time like the present.

"Justin has offered to be my donor," Taylor blurted before she could wimp out. Bruce went limp with relief as she added, "We did the initial tests yesterday and have a meeting set up with a local donor this afternoon so that she can tell us her story."

Taylor expected her mother to be overjoyed, but Caroline's eyes narrowed as she turned to Justin. "If you're just saying you want to donate so that you can trick my daughter into being with you—"

"Mom!" Taylor cut her off, horrified. "How can you say that?"

But Justin didn't share her fury. Instead, in as

steady and genuine a voice as she'd ever heard, he said, "I love your daughter with all my heart, Mrs. Cardenes, and there's nothing I wouldn't do for her. *Nothing.*"

Her mother stared at him, her expression unreadable for several long moments. Finally, she said, "When will you know if you're a match?" Already, despite her reservations about Justin, the fervent hope that Taylor had been worried about was written all over her face.

"Within the next couple of days, I hope. Depending on how well staffed the UC Davis lab is this weekend, however, we may have to wait until Monday."

Silently, Bruce got up to leave the three of them alone to hash things out.

"Given your new relationship with one another," her mother said, "how are you going to deal with your job in Germany? I can't imagine the distance would be a help in either case."

"Mom, please." Taylor didn't think Twenty Questions was fair right now—or ever.

But Justin didn't seem at all perturbed. "I'm already working with my brother Grant to look for a nearby lab to set up operations as soon as possible. He's actually driving up to look at a couple of good options this afternoon before heading to a meeting in the East Bay."

Taylor knew that Justin had planned to make the location change, but she hadn't realized how quickly the other Morrisons would step in to help. Then again, they'd always operated as a team—one she felt immensely honored to become a part of, as Justin's siblings looked out for her the way they'd always looked out for each other.

But before Taylor could express her gratitude at the hours Grant was putting in on Justin's—and on her—behalf, her mother had yet another probing question for him. "Once you move your business here from Germany, where will you live?"

"With me." Taylor didn't think before speaking, but once she said it, she realized she shouldn't be making decisions for Justin, especially when she had repeatedly asked him not to make them for her. "What I meant to say," she said as she turned to face him, "is that I'd love it if you wanted to move in with me. I know my cottage isn't very big, and that you might want a place of your own, so I don't want you to feel pressured or anything."

"Of course I want to move in with you. The only reason I hadn't suggested it already is because I didn't want to pressure *you*."

"Pressure, shmessure," Caroline said. Taylor had almost forgotten her mother was still in the room. "If the two of you are going to be exchanging kidneys, then moving in together is hardly a big deal."

That was when Taylor realized they had skipped

past one very important detail. "The thing is, Mom, even if Justin does end up being a match, I don't know if I'm going to let him go through with it."

"Are you crazy?" Her mother jumped out of her seat. *"Of course* you're going to let Justin donate his kidney to you!"

This was exactly what Taylor had wanted to avoid. But though her stomach was twisted in knots, she couldn't back down at the first hurdle. Not if she was going to prove to her mother—and to herself—that her days of being afraid to make her own decisions were over.

"I'm still trying to figure out how I feel about it all," she explained. "And I'm not going to let anyone make me feel guilty for not being sure. This is a super big, super hard decision. One I would never take lightly, even if everyone else thinks it should already be a done deal."

She expected her mother to come right back at her with arguments, with pleas to see reason, to let Justin's donation be a *fait accompli*. Instead, her mom was staring at her as though she was seeing her for the very first time.

Really seeing her.

"All I want is for you to be okay again," Caroline said eventually, the words halting. "To not be sick anymore." Tears fell, but she didn't wipe them away.

"The last thing I want is to make things worse for you, honey. I just want to support you in any way I can. That's why I came. That's why I brought Bruce."

"I know, Mom." Taylor slid across Bruce's empty seat to her mother's side, knowing in her heart that it was finally time to talk about the one thing they'd never spoken of—but desperately needed to. "Emily," she began in a soft voice. "My sister, what was she like?" She gripped her mom's hands. "I know it's hard for you to talk about her, but I've wanted to know for so long."

"Emily was beautiful." Her mother's words were barely above a whisper. "She looked so much like you, but with bright green eyes. And when she laughed…" For a moment, Taylor thought her mother was going to break down. But then, she gave a small smile instead. "Her laughter was one of the most beautiful sounds in the world."

"I wish I could have known her," Taylor said.

"I was only just pregnant with you when she got that fever—the doctor said it was nothing to worry about—" She broke off on a sob.

"Mom, I'm so sorry." Taylor hugged her mother, wishing she could take away her pain.

"Once I had you, and then your brother, I prayed I would never hear another doctor tell me one of you was ill. But I couldn't stop worrying. It's why I always tried to keep you close. To make sure you stayed safe. I was terrified when you moved away, when I couldn't keep watch over you, but the truth is that you've flourished, honey. Flourished without my hovering over you every second. But then…" More tears fell. "How can it be fair? How can you be sick? Wasn't it enough for us to lose Emily? To go through that pain? I would give anything, *anything*, to make you well."

"Mom, you've been amazing." Taylor gently wiped away her mother's tears before drying her own. "Everything is going to be okay." She had said it so many times, but she'd never hoped for it to come true more than she did right at this moment. "And thank you for telling me about my sister."

"I should have talked to you about Emily a long time ago." Her mother was clearly drained from all the emotion. And yet, Taylor couldn't help but think there seemed to be a new strength to her now, perhaps from finally letting the pain of the past go, even if just the slightest bit. "I love you, honey, and no matter what you decide, I'll try to support you. I have to warn you, though, it may not be easy if you make decisions that aren't what I would want you to do. Which is why I reserve the right as your mother to go to the mat with you about pretty much anything."

Despite the tears they'd both just shed, Taylor had to laugh.

"Now," her mother said as she stood abruptly, "since you and Justin already have plenty on your plates, and I know I'll only be in the way if I stay, I'm going to collect Bruce and head back to the airport to get us both on the next flight home. Please, just promise to let me know the test results the moment you get them."

"Of course I will," Taylor said, "but you don't have to go." For all her intent to be strong and grown up, now that Caroline was planning to leave, Taylor suddenly felt like a little girl again. One who wanted to cling to her mom for dear life.

"Don't worry, your father and I are planning to come out for a long visit in the near future. But for now, I can see that you have everything well in hand. And Justin—" He had risen at the same time, and she reached out to clasp his hands in hers. "I may not always have been your biggest fan, but I can see you genuinely care for my daughter. Thank you."

"You're the one I need to thank," he said, his voice slightly gruff. "You raised an incredible woman. You and your husband should be very proud."

"We are." Caroline pulled Taylor into her arms, and as they held each other, Taylor felt closer to her mother than ever before.

Ten minutes later, when her mom and her ex were on their way back to San Francisco, Taylor sank onto the couch. "That was exhausting."

"And awesome." Justin put his hands on either side of her face and kissed her once—softly, sweetly. "You really impressed your mom when you told her it was time to let go."

"I'm afraid I hurt her."

"You didn't. At least, not in the long term. I can't believe that she would have raised a strong, independent woman to be anything but exactly that." His phone dinged in his pocket. "It's time to meet with the donor."

He didn't ask if she was up for it, and she appreciated that he didn't. If he was certain that she was strong enough to deal with what came next, no matter how difficult, then she was going to do her best to believe it too.

CHAPTER SIXTEEN

Justin didn't try to liven up their drive today the way he had when they'd gone to UC Davis. He was still gunning to be Taylor's donor, but she clearly needed a little time to process. Especially after her mother and ex-boyfriend's unexpected visit this morning.

If he could have rescheduled this meeting, he would have. But speaking with a donor was an important part of the evaluation process, and the transplant center wouldn't let him proceed until he'd talked with at least one. Plus, he really hoped that hearing what the donor had to say would help Taylor wrap her head around him helping her this way.

"Before we go inside," Taylor said after Justin had parked the car, "I just want to make sure that if hearing this woman's story gives you any doubts about donating a kidney to me—for any reason at all—you'll promise to tell me."

It was on the tip of his tongue to say, yet again, that he didn't have any doubts and that nothing could possibly change his mind. But knowing that wouldn't help his cause, he simply said, "I will." And, of course, he had to kiss her. A soft and sweet but also deliciously sexy kiss. He hoped it would help settle her nerves. Or, at the very least, give her something else to focus on.

"You're amazing, Justin." He was glad to see a small smile playing on her lips. "Here I am freaking out about everything—and then, with one kiss, you make me almost forget what I was worried about in the first place."

"Almost?" He brought her mouth back to his so that he could whisper against her lips, "Hopefully, this one will make you *completely* forget."

God, how he loved the little sounds of pleasure she made. If they were anywhere else, at any other time, he would have driven away to find a place where they could see their passion all the way through. But the dinging from his phone was an insistent reminder that pleasure would have to wait a little while.

Taylor fixed her hair with the help of the mirror on the visor. "What are the odds she was looking out the front window and saw us making out?"

Thankfully, from the amused tone of Taylor's voice, she didn't seem particularly worried about it. "I don't know about her," Justin said, "but I'm thinking that guy over there certainly enjoyed the show." He was grinning as he pointed to a man raking leaves at the far end of the street.

"And to think that my mother wasn't always your biggest fan, when you're always such a good influence on me," she teased as they got out of the car.

Hand in hand, they walked up the stone steps. Taylor rang the doorbell, and seconds later, a petite woman with dark brown hair and bright blue eyes opened the door. "Welcome! I'm Debra, and I'm really glad you both could come meet with me today."

"Thank you for meeting with us, Debra. I'm Justin Morrison, and this is my girlfriend, Taylor Cardenes."

They both shook her hand, and then she led them inside her home, a striking contemporary with a vineyard behind it.

"Your home is beautiful," Taylor said, taking in the floor-to-ceiling windows and gleaming wood floors.

"Thank you. My husband and I just finished remodeling. For most of the past year, we've lived in the barn out back." She pointed to the barn, which had been converted with large windows throughout. "I run my candlemaking business out of it, so it's good to have a little separation between work and play now."

"I'm sure you're busy," Taylor said with a nervous smile, "and we don't want to keep you too long…"

Waving away Taylor's concern, Debra said, "I'm always happy to meet with anyone the Davis transplant center sends my way." She gestured for them to come sit down in a sunroom. "I just made this lemon-ade from the Meyer lemons in my garden." She poured them each a glass, and Taylor took a big gulp before setting it down.

"How about I tell you my story," Debra said, "and then you can ask whatever questions you like."

"That would be great." Justin held Taylor's hand firmly in his. He could feel her trembling, just enough that only he could tell.

"My friend Maya was like you, Taylor. She was the picture of health—vibrant, pretty, with no outward signs that anything was wrong. We were roommates ten years ago, and sometimes she would stay in on the weekends, saying she'd had a hard week at work and just wanted to chill, but there was never anything that made me suspect she was unwell. Not until I came home early from a business trip and found her on the couch, crying. You have to understand, she was one of the toughest people I'd ever met, so I knew something was wrong. Really wrong. That's when it all came spilling out, that she had PKD and her kidneys were shutting down. She was weeks away from dialysis, and she was scared. Not only about the disease, but also because she didn't feel she had any other options." Debra paused to take a shaky breath. "I'm sorry, even now, when I think back to how sad, how lost she was. I get all choked up."

"Please," Taylor said, "don't apologize for any-thing."

"We can't tell you how much we appreciate your opening up your home to us and telling your story." Justin squeezed Taylor's hand. "Especially since I know exactly how you felt that day. I only found out about Taylor's diagnosis this week."

"There's nothing like realizing that all that time, someone you love has been getting sicker and sicker, and you didn't even know," Debra agreed. "When I asked Maya how she could have been so ill without telling any of us, or asking for help, she told me she didn't want to ask anyone she knew for a kidney. That it was too much, too big a favor to ask of anyone she loved. We argued about it, of course. I told her I would get tested immediately, even though she told me not to. And when it turned out that I was a match, and I insisted on donating a kidney to her, there was some yelling and crying—but in the end, she realized I was serious, that I wouldn't even freak out about having to write a will before the procedure."

"Wait, what did you just say?" Taylor's eyes were huge. "You had to write a *will*?"

Debra nodded. "Every living donor has to know there is a risk that they might not wake up from the surgery. It's a tiny risk, of course, but you can't ignore it."

"Taylor," Justin said, "the risks of surgery are the last thing I'm afraid of."

Debra looked between the two of them, obviously taking stock of the situation. "Half the time, when people come to see me and hear my story, it's the potential donors who are unsure about taking this step. But the other half of the time, it's the people who need the transplant who are deeply conflicted." She looked at Taylor. "I take it you're having misgivings about allowing Justin to donate his kidney to you?"

"When I was first diagnosed," Taylor said, "and I started to read through the material my doctors gave me about living donors, it made me so queasy to think about anyone making that sacrifice for me that I never actually got all the way through it." Her face was pale as she added in a hollow voice, "I had no idea about the will."

"I'm not going to lie to you," Debra said. "It can be tough for both parties. My parents were…" She paused to search for the right word. "Let's just say they weren't exactly pleased with my decision. My mother must have found every horror story out there, every transplant that had ever gone wrong. On the plus side," she added with a quirk of her lips, "I definitely knew what I was getting myself into."

"Did you ever want to walk away?" Taylor asked.

"Sure." Perhaps Justin shouldn't be happy that

Debra sounded so matter-of-fact about it, but he was glad she wasn't pulling any punches. The more information Taylor had, the better, even if all of it wasn't sunshine and roses. "I'm not a huge fan of hospitals or needles," Debra told them. "And in the middle of the night, those horror stories my mother found kind of got to me."

"But you went through with it anyway?" Taylor sounded as though she could barely believe it.

"There have been a few times in my life when I knew something was right," Debra explained. "Falling in love with my husband. Having my kids. Starting my business. And helping Maya—it was one hundred percent the right thing to do, and I've never regretted it."

"But what if you get sick one day?" Taylor asked. "What if your remaining kidney fails?"

"If that happens, I'll just have to hope someone will come along to help me the way I helped her."

"What about Maya?"

"She's doing well," Debra said with a smile. "At least, she was the last time we talked."

"Are you not close anymore? Even after you gave her a kidney?"

"Don't get me wrong, she's still super grateful. No birthday or anniversary or holiday passes without lavish gifts for me and my husband and kids. Too lavish, if you ask me. But just like everyone else, our lives are busy. I'm here, she's in Paris, and we both have our own families and businesses. We've seen each other when we can over the years, but she knows I'm not expecting her to be beholden to me for the rest of time. If I wasn't willing to donate without strings attached, then I shouldn't have done it." Debra turned her focus to Justin. "You've been pretty quiet over there."

"As a scientist," he said, "I prefer cut and dried, black and white, yes and no. But the deeper I go into all of this with Taylor, the more I can see that it's a complicated situation."

"For both of you," Debra agreed. "One minute you're confident, the next you're scared out of your mind. Hope turns to doubt in an instant, and then back again, like you're on a merry-go-round that's spinning out of control."

"That's exactly how I feel," Taylor said. "Up then down, forward then back, inside then out. I mean, I'm stuck in this situation no matter what, but Justin isn't. And when I think of the risks…"

Debra reached out to put a hand over Taylor's. "I wish I had the magic words to make it less confusing. I don't, but if you have any more questions at any point, I'm just down the road."

"Thank you." Justin and Taylor laughed as they

both spoke at the same time, then stood to say their good-byes.

"I hope you'll accept a little gift from me," Debra said, handing them each a candle at the front door.

Taylor lifted hers to her nose to inhale a slightly spicy mix of lavender and rosemary. Justin's smelled just as good, like freshly picked lavender. "They smell incredible, and I love their shape. It looks so organic."

"Since I use natural ingredients for my molds, they break down a little bit with each candle. I figure since nothing is perfect," Debra said, "there's no point in pretending. Not even with candles." She gave each of them a spontaneous hug. "I know it might not be easy, but something tells me you two are going to come out of this okay. Good luck."

Justin was feeling good about their visit as they walked to the car and got in. Debra hadn't painted a perfectly rosy picture, by any means, but overall, it was obvious that no matter how she weighed the pros and cons, even with the distance of time, the positives of her experience far outweighed the negatives. It was, he hoped, exactly what Taylor needed to hear.

"I can't do this anymore."

On the verge of pulling out onto the street, Justin put the car into park and looked at Taylor with alarm. "What do you mean? Did something Debra said freak you out?"

"You mean in addition to the whole making a will thing?"

That *had* been pretty bad. But he'd assumed Taylor had already read through all of the material on donating. He wouldn't make any more assumptions going forward. "Yeah, something else."

"I don't know." Taylor scrunched her eyes shut and ran her hands over her face. "Actually, I do. From here until tomorrow, can we make a pact not to talk about any of this? Can we just pretend for the next fifteen hours that I'm perfectly healthy and that you're my new boyfriend and we're having a romantic weekend together in the wine country?"

Justin knew time was of the essence. Every phone call made today, every doctor visit, every bit of reading and scheduling and planning could be immeasurably helpful going forward. The opportunity cost of postponing any of it was bigger than he wanted to imagine.

And yet…

He could see how worn down Taylor was by it all—and he also knew that the additional stress couldn't possibly be helping. So even though it went against every last one of his science-based instincts, if it was romance she needed tonight, he vowed that romance was exactly what she would get.

CHAPTER SEVENTEEN

Taylor was glad for the routine of setting up and serving afternoon tea for her guests. Making a batch of cookies, pouring wine, having a little light conversation, giving sightseeing tips and recommendations—it was all so *normal*. For an hour, she could be a B&B owner with not a care in the world other than making sure her guests were happy and her business was thriving.

Justin made himself scarce for most of the afternoon, and though even a handful of hours without him made her miss him—how had she made it through five years?—she knew he must need some time to decompress. They hadn't spoken about his mini-breakdown in the shower last night, but she couldn't forget the shaking of his broad shoulders as he'd bowed his head, held on to her, and finally given himself a break from being a pillar of strength and let some tears fall.

Today, nothing Debra said had seemed to faze him, but surely he must have some doubts, even if they were tiny. Then again, she seemed to have doubts enough for both of them. So many that she'd been unable to hold in yet another freak-out in the car after their meeting…

Her guests had all gone out to dinner in town by the time she finished washing and putting away the last of the teacups, wine glasses, and champagne flutes. She loved her B&B when it was bustling with happy voices, but tonight she was more than ready to head back to her cottage, draw a bath, and read a book. Whenever Justin got back, she'd welcome him with open arms and apologize for her totally unreasonable request—no matter how much she wished they could pretend that they were having a romantic weekend in the wine country, they couldn't. One day maybe they'd be able to steal that time together, but for now she had to accept that doctor visits and medical tests took priority over everything else.

As she headed through the garden to her cottage, she was so preoccupied with her incessantly swirling thoughts and worries that she barely noticed the sun was just starting to set and the moon was rising on the opposite side of the sky. Even drawing a bath and sinking beneath the bubbles hardly soothed her, although it did help the ache in her side recede a bit.

If Justin were here, he'd know exactly what to say and do. He'd figure out a way to make her laugh. And he'd surely set out to make her knees weak too.

Longing for him even more now than before, she forcefully reminded herself that Justin already had to deal with a sick girlfriend—the last thing he needed was for her to become desperate and clingy, unable to function without him. That wasn't the woman she wanted to be. And she was certain that wasn't the woman he had fallen in love with.

Love. Justin's love made her feel more lucky than she'd ever been, even when in many ways her luck had never been worse. She wanted him to feel just as lucky, which was another reason she couldn't let every second they spent together be about her disease.

She'd said she wanted romance, but she hadn't done anything to make it happen, had she?

Just that quickly, an idea came to her—the *perfect* romantic plan.

Napa Valley was one of the most romantic places on earth. Thousands of proposals had been made in her town, thousands of brides and grooms had proclaimed their never-ending love to each other in nearby vineyards and wineries. All these years, Taylor had longed for the chance to be with Justin, and she wanted to make sure they celebrated fantasy becoming beautiful reality.

After getting out of the tub and wrapping a towel around herself, she called her friend Angie to ask if she could cover breakfast in the morning. Taylor hadn't planned to miss two breakfasts in her first week at the B&B, but these were extenuating circumstances.

Her next call was to a company that she never thought she'd actually work with. If only because she'd never been particularly good with heights. Of all the scary things she was facing lately, however, heights barely made the list.

She had only just disconnected and set the alarm on her phone for four thirty a.m. when Justin walked in. "Anyone home?"

"I'm in the bedroom."

His eyes lit up—then went dark with heat—when he saw she was wearing only a towel. "Damn," he said, "it's good to see you." He looked super yummy in a navy button-down shirt and dark slacks, and she realized he must have showered and shaved in his room at the B&B. He pulled her into his arms. "Are you just getting into the bath or just getting out?"

"Out," she replied, "but I'm more than happy to get back in with you."

He groaned, the sound reverberating from his chest to hers. "I can't tell you how badly I want to do that, but we need to get going."

"Get going? Where?"

"I've made reservations." He smiled at her. "*Romantic* reservations." Of course he had. Because all he wanted was for her to be happy. "But if you're too tired—"

"No, I'm fine." Though she'd been drooping on her feet before, she suddenly felt like a million bucks. All because Justin loved her. "Actually, I feel *great* now that you're here. I just need to get dressed." She opened her antique pine armoire. "Dress code?" Judging by his outfit, she took a guess. "Something pretty?" She held up a green silk dress with long sleeves and a nipped-in waist.

"Perfect. I'll wait in the kitchen while you get ready. Otherwise, I won't be able to resist the allure of taking a bath with you." She had to laugh at the slightly pained look on his face as he walked away.

She would have loved to have climbed into the tub with him, but honestly, the chance to put on makeup and a dress and heels to go out on a date with her boyfriend filled her with a wonderful rush of happiness. It was funny how something small like this could make her feel lighter, more hopeful. She needed to remember this moment as she moved forward over the next weeks, months, and years—that she shouldn't make the mistake of forgetting to appreciate the little things—a sunrise, a smile, a perfect chocolate chip cookie.

And especially a romantic evening out with the man she loved.

He wouldn't tell her where they were going, but that was perfectly okay with Taylor. As long as they were together, she knew it would be great. Even the drive was perfect, the sun having just disappeared behind the mountains, leaving the vineyards glowing in a soft, dusky light.

Twenty minutes later, Justin pulled into the Wine Train parking lot. "Surprise."

"I've been wanting to do this for months!" She threw her arms around him and kissed him. "I love it already."

She could see how pleased he was by her appreciation of his romantic gesture as he grinned and said, "I hope you love it even more once we're on the train."

"Ms. Cardenes, Mr. Morrison, welcome to Romance on the Rails." The conductor, who was wearing a sharp black suit and cap, gave them a bow. "We are very glad you are able to join us tonight on our magical and romantic journey. Please watch your step as you board, and then I will take you to your private dining quarters."

Taylor lifted her eyebrows at Justin. Private dining quarters? She hadn't even realized the Wine Train had such a thing. She'd looked into buying a ticket to one of their murder mysteries a few months back, but had glossed right over their romance package. After all, what was the point in thinking about romance when the only man she cared about was thousands of miles away?

She would have given herself a little pinch to make sure this evening was real if Justin hadn't taken her hand just then. Following the conductor, they passed through one beautiful restored Pullman car after another. There were a few families in the first car, but most of the Wine Train's passengers tonight were couples. Young, old, or somewhere in between, they all looked happy to be on board the luxurious train, and most looked to be deeply in love as well.

But it was hard to imagine any of them could compare with what she and Justin had together. A bond so deep, so true, so strong, that love was blossoming even in the midst of their less-than-perfect situation.

Tonight *was* perfect, though. A romantic trip on the Napa Valley Wine Train was exactly the kind of date she'd been longing for this afternoon when her head was spinning.

The conductor led them into the final car. "You will be dining beneath our glass-topped Vista Dome with the stars twinkling above and panoramic views of the silver-painted vineyards all around you as we traverse Napa Valley tonight. If you will please take a seat, I'd like to present you with one of our finest local vintages, a sparkling wine we hope you will greatly enjoy. And now, please relax and let us know if there is anything we can do to make your romantic evening shine even brighter."

"I know one thing that can definitely be improved upon," Justin said once they were alone. He scooted his chair closer, so that they were sitting side by side instead of on opposite sides of the round dining table, and put his arm around her as the train slowly made its way out of the station. "I would pull you onto my lap, but this looks to be a family-friendly trip." The wicked glint in his eyes gave testament to the fact that he really did want her sitting on his lap.

Blissfully happy, she leaned her head against his shoulder. "This is the perfect escape."

"I agree."

Sitting close, they looked through the windows and the roof as the stars began to appear one by one, almost as though someone were turning them on with a light switch simply to captivate the two of them. Together, they pointed out the constellations they knew and made up names for those they didn't.

Taylor wasn't sure she'd ever seen so many stars. Or maybe it just seemed that way because everything seemed brighter and better when she was with Justin.

"Do you remember that night we snuck past the fence at the Dish and spent the night gazing at stars?" The hiking trails on the edge of the Stanford campus had been named for the massive high-powered antenna that had been installed at the top of the hill in 1962.

"I was just thinking the same thing," he said, pressing a kiss to the top of her head. "I nearly told you that night."

She shifted to look at him. "Told me what?"

"That I loved you. That I'd always loved you. That I always would."

Her heart melted, and when she kissed him, she couldn't hold back. Before she knew it, she actually had started to climb into his lap, family-friendly trip be damned.

The sound of a throat clearing had her jumping back into her seat, cheeks flaming. Justin, on the other hand, looked extremely pleased with himself.

The waiter did an impressive job of keeping a straight face. "Everything we will be serving you tonight is made from local ingredients. To begin, an *amuse-bouche* made of local butternut squash and zucchini."

Taylor's stomach growled, and she realized she'd barely eaten all day. She usually ate breakfast after her guests in the morning, but with her mother and Bruce there, she'd been in a rush to get things worked out with them. And then they'd gone to meet with Debra in Yountville before coming back to put on tea for her guests. Altogether, she'd nibbled only some scrambled eggs in the morning and then half a cookie in the afternoon.

Having promised everyone from Justin to her mother to her doctors that she would take good care of herself, she should dig in. But first she needed Justin to know something. "I nearly did the same thing that night up at the Dish. I was *this close* to blurting out my feelings for you."

"You were?" He looked stunned. "How the hell could I have been so blind? If I'd had even the slightest inkling that you felt the way I did…"

"I've always been good at hiding my feelings, at pushing them away when they feel too big or too hard to deal with." She swallowed hard. "Sometimes, I'm afraid I'm going to fall back into that pattern. Even this afternoon, I was so ready to escape reality that I made you promise to act like none of it is happening, to pretend that everything is sunshine and butterflies and rainbows."

He lifted her hands to his lips and pressed a kiss to each of her palms. "I agree that we shouldn't hide our feelings, and we shouldn't pretend we're not dealing with some massive decisions. But I don't want us to stop seeing sunshine, butterflies, and rainbows either. That's what happened to my dad after my mom died, and I know she wouldn't have wanted to see him like that. And, if I'm being totally honest, that's what happened to me in Frankfurt."

Before she could ask what he meant, the waiter returned with their salads. As soon as they were alone again, she said, "You haven't talked much about Germany, but I thought it was good for you. I thought you were doing work you wanted to do."

"I was. I am." But that spark she was so used to seeing in his eyes dimmed as he told her, "I let it consume me. I was more than happy to let my work, my research, take the place of everything I no longer had. My colleagues were pleased by my fervor and endless energy, at least in the first couple of years."

"Then what happened?" She could see this wasn't easy to talk about, and she was proud of him for doing it anyway.

He stared out the window, but she knew he wasn't seeing the Napa Valley night. "It crept up on me, how tired I felt. How uninspired."

"But you didn't take a break to recharge?"

He shook his head. "My colleagues kept inviting me to join the local soccer team, or to meet up with them at the biergarten. But I couldn't stop thinking about all the work that wouldn't get done. And I kept telling myself we were almost there with our research, that we'd nail it if I just spent a few more hours every day. So I blocked myself off from everyone and everything but the lab and my research and ended up getting grouchy and short with everyone. Sleep eluded me more and more too, and even the things I used to enjoy doing, like hiking and woodworking, lost their pull. My goal to find a cure for breast cancer became my only reason to get up in the morning and the reason I wouldn't let myself go to sleep at night." His expression was grim as he said, "The thing is, it wasn't just about the work. About finding the cure. It was about hiding. From my feelings about losing my mom. And from my feelings about you. Because I knew you would never be mine...and I couldn't stand the thought of a life without you."

"I was hiding too," she admitted. "In my relationship with Bruce. In a job I didn't want. In a life my parents had mapped out for me because otherwise they would worry. It wasn't until I got sick that I had to stop making them my excuse for always playing it safe and being a coward."

"A coward?" He said it as though nothing could be further from the truth. "Do you know what my mother always used to say about you?" When she shook her head, he smiled. "She thought you were the bravest woman in the world to throw yourself into the mix with us Morrisons. And then later, when you would spend all those hours with her in the hospital, she would say it again and again—that you were the only person she wasn't related to who had the guts to come and be with her." Justin lifted his hand to Taylor's cheek. "You were never afraid. And we all loved you more than ever for that. For being there for her when everyone else fled."

"I loved your mom." There were tears in Taylor's eyes, and she had a big lump in her throat. "I wanted to be with her."

"I love you." Justin's words were as sincere as any she'd heard him speak. And then, before she realized it, he was slipping out of his chair, getting down on one knee, and reaching into his pocket for a small, velvet-covered box. "Taylor Cardenes, I've known from the first moment I met you that I wanted you to be mine. Will you marry me?"

CHAPTER EIGHTEEN

Taylor's eyes were huge as she stared at him. He was holding one of her hands, but the other was over her mouth, which had fallen open.

Justin's heart was pounding a million beats a minute. He'd never been so nervous—or felt so certain—about anything in his entire life. They might have been dating only a few days shy of a week, but for eight years, Taylor had been his best friend…and his secret love.

Time, as they both knew all too well, offered no guarantees. And he didn't want to waste any more of it. He wanted Taylor to be his wife and he wanted to be her husband. He wanted to start a family with her as soon as her doctors gave them the thumbs-up. He wanted to help her run her B&B and ask her to look over his work at the lab to see what brilliant insights she had to help move them closer to a cure. He didn't plan on spending nearly as much time in his lab in the future, but he'd be hugely energized and focused during the time he did spend working.

He also finally understood that he would be able to do so much more to make others' lives better if he were living his own life to the fullest. He wanted to spend every Christmas, every birthday, every Valentine's Day with Taylor beside him. He wanted them to be a team in everything, good or bad.

The ring had been burning a hole in his pocket for the past hour. Taylor knew him so well that he was almost surprised she hadn't guessed it was there. He had planned for his proposal to come at the end of the evening, after the food had been cleared and there was no chance of anyone disturbing them. But he hadn't been able to hold it in, not when he could have sworn his mother was whispering in his ear: *Ask her.*

"Yes."

Taylor spoke so softly that Justin wasn't sure he'd heard her correctly. "Yes?" His voice shook with hope and love and longing.

"Yes!" she yelled, flinging her arms around his neck so that the ring box was accidentally knocked out of his hand as she slid from her seat to kneel on the carpet with him.

They kissed like they'd never kissed before. A best-friends-turned-lovers-turned-newly-engaged-couple kiss that blew all the others out of the water.

He never wanted to let her go, but at the same

time, he was anxious to cement their engagement by getting the ring onto her finger. The box was only a few feet away, beneath the window. But when he picked it up, the ring was no longer inside.

Together, they hunted for it on their hands and knees, looking in every crevice, every corner. That was how the wait staff found them, with their rear ends sticking up in the air, their eyes slightly wild.

"We just got engaged," Taylor said.

The man and woman holding the covered trays gave them confused smiles. "Congratulations."

"The ring went flying," Justin explained in what he hoped was a calm voice, but wasn't anywhere close. "That's why we're down here searching for it."

"Not to worry, sir," the waiter said as he put down his tray. "We'll help you."

The four of them crept around the dining car for what was probably only a couple of minutes, but felt far longer, when the other waiter called out, "I found it!" She held it up, and Justin only barely stopped himself from grabbing it out of her hands. "Oh, it's lovely."

"Is it?" Taylor said on a laugh. "I can't wait to see it."

"Forgive me." The woman gave the ring to Justin. "We'll give you two some time alone."

But Justin didn't want to wait another second, and

clearly neither did Taylor, because she thrust her left hand at him so that he could slide the ring into place.

It was a perfect fit. Just as he'd known it would be.

"It's *so* beautiful." Taylor held up her hand so that the diamonds caught the glow of the lights. "I've never seen a ring like it."

He'd been inspired by seeing her in her wine country garden and knowing how right she looked in it. Even though he could easily have afforded something more expensive, he knew she wouldn't feel comfortable in something flashy. So instead of one big diamond, two dozen beautifully cut diamonds radiated out from the center like petals.

It wasn't until Taylor's stomach growled again—which set off the chain reaction of his stomach growling—that he realized they were still on the floor. Laughing, they got up, then seated themselves to eat the food the servers had left for them.

But before they did, he said, "This is now officially the best day of my life."

"For me too," she agreed, linking hands with him.

And as he grinned like a fool at the sight of his ring on her finger, he couldn't help but wonder just how soon they could pull together a wedding.

★ ★ ★

Two hours later, after they had made it home and were

heading through her garden to the cottage, Taylor was still walking on air. She couldn't stop looking at the engagement ring and admiring it—just as she couldn't stop looking at Justin and admiring him too. He was so handsome, so smart, so powerful, so sweet. So all-around wonderful in every single way.

She had been stunned by his proposal, but not only for the reasons he must have thought. What he wouldn't know until tomorrow morning was that—

Out of the blue, at the threshold of her cottage, he swept her up into his arms and kissed her breathless, making all thoughts fall from her brain. "We're not married yet," she teased once she could form words again.

"A guy can dream, can't he?"

She caressed his cheek as he carried her over the threshold. "The whole night was like a dream. Thank you for such sweet romance."

"It's what you've always deserved." He set her down in the living room, her body sizzling from making the slow slide against his. "I'm sorry I haven't given you more romance before tonight."

"You've always given me what I needed. If we had gotten together back in college, honestly, I'm not sure that I would have been ready for the passion between us...or for how big you make my heart feel." She had needed some time to mature, to come into her own and figure out what she really wanted out of life. "All those years, I got to love you from a safe distance. If you had given me romance back then, I probably would have freaked out and run."

"Then I guess I'm glad I didn't, because I would hate for you ever to run from me." He put his hands on either side of her face and looked into her eyes. "You'll tell me if I'm coming on too strong, won't you? If I'm moving too fast?"

Again, she thought about how surprised he was going to be in the morning when he found out that he wasn't the only one who had been moving fast. She was tempted to tell him now, but she didn't want to spoil what she hoped would be another really lovely and romantic moment.

"Trust me," she said, "we're in perfect sync." In every single way…

Their lips were nearly touching when her cell phone and the landline in the cottage both rang at the same time. She frowned as she reluctantly pulled away from him. "That must be one of my guests. I hope nothing is wrong."

But she soon found out there was. The couple who had checked in that afternoon, then headed out to drive through the mountains of Calistoga, had blown a tire on their rental car. The manual was missing from the glove box and they couldn't find the spare. They'd called the rental company, but they had no cars left on the lot. And when they'd called their auto service hotline, they were told there was a backup of several hours.

"I've got to go pick them up," she said.

"I'll come too."

Taylor knew there would be many more wonderful nights with Justin, especially now that they were engaged. Still, she couldn't help regretting that they couldn't yet celebrate their engagement.

He seemed to read her mind. "Before you know it, we'll be back here, warming each other up in your bathtub."

She gave him a quick kiss, told him where to find the pump and patch kit in the garage, then went to change into jeans and a jacket. She thought briefly about taking off her ring—she'd hate for anything to happen to it while she was helping with the tires. But that was a risk she was going to have to take.

Now that Justin had put his ring on her finger, she never, ever wanted to take it off.

* * *

Four hours later, they finally made it back to her B&B. Her guests had been beyond thankful that they'd not only come to help them, but had also brought warm blankets and a flask of hot cider. After tucking them into the backseat of her car, Taylor and Justin had gone to see what could be done about the tire.

As much as the previous part of their evening had been magical and perfect, the next was one long string of errors. Once they found the spare, the security lug-nut tool that should have been with it was missing, so they couldn't loosen the nuts to take off the flat tire. It was sheer luck that a county road maintenance worker came along in his service truck with an air compressor and a plug kit, and could repair the tire enough to get them down the hill to St. Helena.

The sun hadn't yet started to rise, but it would soon. It was tempting to fall into bed to catch a little sleep before morning officially came. Taylor felt as though she was buzzing inside, which tended to happen when she was just on the borderline of exhaustion. But she desperately wanted to give Justin the same magical romance he'd given her just hours ago.

She wouldn't make a habit of pulling all-nighters, but just this once surely couldn't hurt. Fortunately, though her side still ached, she hadn't had another full-on burst of pain in the past few days. After she gave him her surprise this morning, she'd be careful not to push her body any harder. After all, she had promised Justin that she knew her limits, and she wanted him to know that he could always trust her.

"I know you're going to think I'm crazy," she said,

"but I have a surprise for you. One that involves taking the world's quickest shower to get the grease off and then getting straight back in the car."

"Of course I want to see what your surprise is," he said, "but are you sure you're up for whatever it is? I'd never forgive myself if I ran you ragged."

"I'm fine," she promised him. "And I really think you'll love my surprise."

His smile made her heart dance around. "Life is never going to be boring with you, is it?"

In her old life, where she'd always followed someone else's step-by-step plans for the future, there had never been many chances to be spontaneous. But as the owner of a wine country B&B, she could see that each day would be wildly different from the next.

And she loved it.

"I sure hope not," she agreed.

After they'd quickly washed their hair and cleaned the grease off their skin—rather than all the other naughty things they would have rather done in the shower—they dashed back out to her car. The sun wasn't up yet, but they could see a glimmer of light just beginning to peek over the hills.

Justin's grin was huge as she turned off the ignition a quarter of an hour later. "We're going up in a hot air balloon?" He looked like an excited kid, and her heart melted all over again. "This is going to be awesome!"

The Morrisons were so adventurous that she was surprised he'd never been up in a hot air balloon before. Especially given that the wine country was only a couple of hours away from Palo Alto. But maybe he'd been waiting to take the flight with her, just as she couldn't help but feel that she'd been waiting to take a trip on the Wine Train with him. There were so many wonderful things she wanted to experience with him— this was only the tip of the iceberg.

A shadow of doubt crept inside before she could block it out. Doubt that she'd be well enough in the future for too many big adventures. Doubt that he'd be a match. Doubt that even if he *was* a match, she could reconcile herself to the idea of him sacrificing so much for her.

She forcefully shook off the dark thoughts. They were here for Romance Part Two. She wouldn't allow her diagnosis, and all the uncertainties that came along with it, to thwart even a single second.

They got out of the car and were soon being given information about their flight—where they'd be flying, at what altitude, and how to stay safe while in the basket beneath the balloon. She'd arranged for an exclusive two-person trip. One of the staff members would be on board as the pilot, but the owner had assured her over the phone that his pilots were masters at fading into the background when necessary.

Not that she had been planning to do anything blush-worthy with Justin up there—but she did have a very special moment planned. Though things had changed since last night, she still wanted to go ahead with it.

Soon, they were climbing into the large basket and setting off into the sky. Justin put his arms around her from behind, and Taylor leaned back into him while they soared in time to the rising sun. The grapevines below undulated over the hills and valleys, a picture-perfect wine country scene in the breathtakingly beautiful early morning light.

They might not have had any sleep, but Taylor felt more crisp and clear than ever before. And despite the darkness that had tried to creep in earlier, she felt so calm now, as though nothing could ever go wrong again.

"Justin." She turned so that they were facing each other and his hands were in hers. "Eight years ago when we met, I knew my life had just changed forever. I couldn't imagine not seeing your smile, and I didn't want to go even a day without hearing your laughter. I knew I'd always be head over heels for you, but what I didn't know was that you'd end up feeling the same way about me too. Yesterday, when you asked me to marry you, you must have been wondering why it took me a few seconds to say yes." She moved closer to him. "It isn't because I had any doubts at all. Of course I don't, even if neither of us can know for sure what's coming in the future." Again, she forced away the dark clouds that kept trying to creep in and let herself focus only on the man she loved. "The reason I was so surprised is because I was planning to propose to you. Here. Now." She laughed. "But you beat me to it."

He kissed her first, then said, "I love you, Taylor. So damned much I swear my heart feels as big as this balloon over our heads."

She reached into the bag she'd brought with her, then held out a velvet box that matched the one he'd given her last night. "I can't wait to marry you. Until then, I hope you'll wear my ring."

His grin was a mile wide as he opened the box, but when he saw the ring inside, he looked like he was about to tear up. "My mom would have loved this ring. *I* love this ring."

Taylor still couldn't believe she'd been able to find a man's band inset with a fire opal. It was simply meant to be.

She lifted it out of the box and slid it onto Justin's ring finger. There was no officiant, no family or friends nearby, no rose-covered arches or cake to cut, but as they soared through the sky wearing each other's rings, Taylor felt as though they'd already made every vow that counted.

From this moment forward, they would love and protect each other through whatever came. She would just have to pray that it would be more good than bad. And trust that even if it wasn't, their love would survive.

CHAPTER NINETEEN

There was no time for a nap when they returned to the B&B. After thanking Angie for stepping in at the last second for breakfast, Taylor found that her cleaning staff had an emergency elsewhere and couldn't come. Justin insisted on helping to scrub bathrooms and change sheets and vacuum, but when his sister called to let him know that they actually did need his help setting up for the rehearsal dinner that night, Taylor insisted that he go.

It was hard to believe that the wedding was tomorrow, she thought as she took a breather on the foot of the king bed in one of the upstairs suites. Where had the week gone?

The mattress and duvet that she'd picked out for this room were so soft and cozy that she was tempted to curl up and take a little nap. But not only would the rooms not clean themselves, she also had treats to bake for afternoon tea and a mountain of paperwork to get through before Justin came back to collect her for the rehearsal dinner.

Thankfully, all she needed to perk up her flagging energy was to look down at the beautiful engagement ring sparkling on her finger. She finished cleaning and then moved on to baking, and every time the sunlight caught in the petal-shaped diamonds, she was surprised and delighted all over again.

Justin would be telling his family this afternoon— and she hoped they'd be happy that she would soon be joining their family. The only one she was worried about, to be honest, was his father.

She couldn't imagine Michael Morrison would be happy to hear that one of his sons was marrying a woman with kidney disease. Not after the family had already been through so much with Lisa's illness and death.

Taylor had been planning to call her parents immediately after the hot air balloon ride, but when her mom texted to say that they were heading down to Saratoga Springs for the weekend to a little B&B they'd been to for their honeymoon, she decided her call could wait. She couldn't remember her parents ever doing anything for themselves—everything had always been about Taylor and her brother. Their talk yesterday had helped Taylor feel better about things. Maybe it had helped her mother too—enough that she was off to have a romantic weekend with her husband for the first time in nearly thirty years.

Before she knew it, the afternoon had wound down, Taylor had given all of her guests restaurant recommendations, and it was time for her to get ready for Drew and Ashley's rehearsal dinner. She longed for a bath, but she'd likely fall asleep in the warm water. Thankfully, after forcing herself into a briskly cool shower, she felt much more bright-eyed and bushy-tailed.

Justin walked into the cottage just as she was putting the finishing touches on her makeup at the antique table in her bedroom.

"I keep thinking I'm going to get used to how beautiful you are." She was wearing pink silk tonight, her dress cut in a figure-hugging style that flattered her curves while not giving away any intimate secrets. "But it's never going to happen."

"I feel exactly the same way." He was beyond gorgeous in a dark suit. So gorgeous that she was sorely tempted to peel the fabric off his broad shoulders. "How did I ever get so lucky?"

He moved behind her in the mirror, and as she looked at the two of them together, she felt like a princess who had miraculously found her prince.

"Something tells me you're going to get even luckier after dinner tonight," he told her in a husky voice as he held out his hand to help her up.

She slipped on her heels, grabbed her purse, and then they headed out through her garden to the car. "What did everyone say when you told them we were engaged?"

"They're thrilled."

"Even your father?"

He looked at her like she was nuts for even asking. "He wasn't there this afternoon, but I know he'll be overjoyed by the news when we tell him tonight. And honestly," he continued, "none of them seemed particularly surprised. In fact, I'd say there was plenty of credit-taking going on, given that they all conspired to book my week here."

"I hope Ashley and Drew don't feel as though we're trying to overshadow their special day." Maybe it was lack of sleep that had her worrying about everything so much right now.

"If you ask me, they were the happiest of all. Two giddy people in love *always* think everyone else should be in love too. And to be honest, I get that now." He shot her a devious look. "Wouldn't it be great if we could figure out how to get Grant to fall for someone? Especially if it's the last woman he ever thought he would fall for."

"It sure would," she agreed. "But what about Olivia and Maddie? Don't you want to see them fall in love too?"

His mouth flattened into a stubborn line that she couldn't help but find cute. "No one will ever be good enough for them."

"You're going to have to stop protecting them at some point, you know."

"Nope," he said, pretending to put his fingers in his ears. "Not listening."

Clearly, this was an argument for another day. Good thing his sisters had her and Ashley and Serena on their side. Otherwise, who knew what shenanigans the Morrison brothers would pull to keep them forever locked up in chastity belts? Taylor knew firsthand how overrated *safe* was.

The venue Ashley and Drew had chosen for their rehearsal dinner was extraordinary. Rather than booking a private room in the back of a restaurant, they had found a wine cellar that had been carved into the mountain, with large windows on one end that looked over a pond that reflected the rising moon.

And yet, even though the beauty of her surroundings was undeniable, Taylor still couldn't settle her nerves. Not even when Justin's brothers and sisters embraced her with open arms as soon as they stepped into the cellar.

"Congratulations!" Maddie cried.

"We always knew you two would end up together one day," Olivia stated with a huge smile on her face.

"I'm so happy that I'm going to have another great sister-in-law soon," Sean said as he bear-hugged her.

"And can I just say how happy I am to know that there's another woman out there I can call when my own Morrison twin is making my head spin?" Serena said with an affectionate eyeroll in Sean's direction.

"You know you love the way I make your head spin," Sean said, giving her a kiss clearly intended to make his point.

Drew and Ashley hugged her as a pair. "We're so happy for you."

"You're both so sweet," Taylor said, "but I feel bad about coming in with our news when this weekend is supposed to be all about you two."

"Are you kidding? Your engagement has made our wedding weekend even more epic!" Taylor was relieved to see that Drew genuinely meant it. "And now that we've got the love vibes really cooking," he said as Grant walked over, "I'm thinking it's time to set our sights on some of the bigger holdouts in the family. Cupid's arrow is unavoidable, you know."

Grant seemed not to hear—clearly, he had a great deal of practice in not letting himself be wound up by his siblings. He leaned over to give Taylor a kiss on the cheek. "It's great to see you, Taylor. Justin gave us the good news earlier. Congratulations. We're all very happy for you both."

She believed he meant it, but she could also see a hint of reserve in his eyes. "Would you mind if we talked privately for a moment?" she asked.

"Sure." Ever the gentleman, he asked if she would be too cold talking outside. When she said she would be just fine, he led her into a private corner of the garden.

"I know you must have some questions about how quickly Justin and I got engaged," she made herself say despite her nerves.

"Not at all," Grant replied before she could say anything more. "You've been a part of our family for nearly a decade. The truth is that we've always hoped you and Justin would become more than friends."

"That's a lovely thing for you to say." The Morrisons were all protective of each other, but Taylor knew that Grant, as the oldest, looked out for his siblings with an eagle eye. "I promise you, I won't ever do anything to hurt him." She couldn't leave it there, though. "Not intentionally." She clasped her hands in front of her to try to stop their shaking.

"You're cold. We should go in."

"Not yet. I know you must have terribly mixed feelings about the idea of Justin donating his kidney to me. And I want you to know that I do too. If it turns out that he's a match, I don't know what I'll do. Because I could never live with myself if anything happened to him."

He stared at her for a long moment. Taylor knew that Grant was never one to make flash judgments or jump to conclusions. He looked at everything from as many angles as possible before making decisions—decisions that were nearly always the right ones. She could hardly breathe as she waited for his response. What if he thought it would be selfish of her to accept Justin's offer?

"None of us can make Justin's decision for him. Nor can we make yours." He was as serious as she'd ever seen him. "But I want you to know that I understand why he wants to give you one of his kidneys. If I were in his shoes, I believe I would do the same thing."

Relief swamped her. A beat later, however, she realized relief had come too soon.

"I didn't want you to come here tonight unaware of the fact that my father is having a tough time with it, though."

She swallowed hard. "Of course he is."

"I don't believe he'll actively stand in Justin's way," Grant said, "but at this point, I'm not sure he's ready to support him either."

Suddenly, Taylor felt every minute of the sleep she'd missed. Her skin felt dry and tight, her limbs heavy, and she had to fight the urge to weep.

"I won't let him do it." She couldn't stand the

thought of coming between Justin and his father. "I'll find another donor, but even if I don't, I won't let my situation pull Justin and your father apart."

Grant put his hand on her arm as though to soothe her, but she barely noticed. "Dad just needs some time to get used to the idea."

"No." She'd been right in the beginning when she'd told Justin she couldn't let him be her donor. "I need to tell your father that even if Justin is a match, I won't let him go into surgery. I won't risk anything happening to him."

"Taylor—" Grant stepped in front of her before she could dash into the cellar to find Michael Morrison. "None of us are going to be able to keep Justin from doing what he wants to do, what he believes is right. He loves you, and he'll do anything for you. And it seems to me that rejecting a donation from him would have as many risks as saying yes. Maybe even more, since he'll never forgive himself if your health takes a turn for the worse and he could have done something to stop it but didn't. Our father just needs some time. He knows how much you mean to Justin and how much Justin means to you. He also knows how much you loved our mother and how much she loved you." It was the most she'd ever heard Grant say at one time, the most impassioned speech she'd ever heard from him. "Grief can make a person blind sometimes," he added in a rough voice, "but he'll come around. Can you trust me on that?"

She knew what Grant wanted her to say. And even though she'd sworn she wouldn't follow other people's plans for her life anymore, she couldn't stand the thought of spoiling Ashley and Drew's wedding weekend.

She nodded and forced her lips up into what she hoped was a convincing smile. "I've always trusted you, Grant. You're the best big brother Justin could ever have." Feeling tears about to rush in again, she gave him a hug. "I'm just going to pop into the ladies' room for a second. See you back inside."

Thankfully, it was a large private room, complete with a small daybed that she could sit on while she put her head in her hands and tried not to feel as though everything had just gone terribly, horribly wrong.

CHAPTER TWENTY

Justin hadn't wanted to believe this could happen, but he wasn't blind.

His father had been avoiding Taylor all night. He'd neither congratulated them on their engagement, nor come over just to say hello. And Justin didn't think it was a coincidence that Drew and Ashley had set up the seating so that Justin and Taylor were on one end of the long table and his father was at the other. Everyone obviously knew Dad had issues with his intention to donate a kidney to Taylor.

What's more, Justin couldn't miss how subdued Taylor had been after returning from her private talk with Grant. She'd looked pale and guilty, when she had absolutely nothing to feel guilty about. Based on a couple of conversations Justin and Grant had had during the week, he knew Grant was prepared to support his decision to be her donor. The only person Justin *hadn't* been able to talk things through with was his father—he'd left messages, but none had been returned.

Earlier, when she'd asked him about his father's reaction to their engagement, Justin had still been firmly in denial about the possibility that he might not support his relationship with Taylor. But that was because he honestly couldn't believe that his father would turn on her out of fear.

Justin had been gritting his teeth all through dinner. He didn't want to make a scene and ruin Drew and Ashley's celebration—but that didn't mean he would let his father leave without talking with him either.

The evening should have been great. The food looked fantastic, and his siblings and Ashley's parents were in top form with alternately funny or heartwarming stories about the bride and groom. But Justin couldn't enjoy himself. Not when he could see that Taylor was trying so hard to act like nothing was wrong, with a smile pasted on her face as she laughed in all the right places. He held tightly to her hand, but she wouldn't look at him.

Somehow, he made it through dinner and dessert and what seemed to be an endless number of toasts. As soon as everyone started to get up from the table, he gave Taylor a kiss, told her he'd be right back, then made a beeline for his father.

"We need to talk."

He didn't wait for a response as he headed out of

the cave, past the stone patio, and into the first row of vines. The smell of the soil beneath his feet and the crisp night air should have filled him with pleasure. But just as he'd been unable to appreciate the meal and the company tonight, he couldn't ground himself in the beauty of the land either.

"Justin." His father's voice had him turning, jaw clenched. "I know you love her, but—"

"Do you?" Fury whipped through Justin as he glared at the man who had always been his hero. "Do you really know how much I love Taylor?" The two of them had never talked about his mother—not really, not in anything more than tiny little remembrances that didn't come anywhere near the heart of their loss. But Justin was done trying to hide from his grief—and he sure as hell wasn't going to allow his father to use his own grief as some sort of weapon against Taylor. "Do you understand that I love her as much as you loved Mom? I know you would have done the same for Mom, with no hesitation at all."

"Of course I would have," his father replied. "But your mother and I were together for more than thirty years. Whereas, while you and Taylor have known each other since college, you've only been a couple for a week."

Justin was momentarily speechless, unable to believe that his father would try to pull out the equivalent of a time calculator, or a ruler to measure love, to judge the amount of time appropriate before you could help someone you loved.

"You always said you fell in love with Mom the day you met." Justin's voice was low, but hard. Never in a million years would he have thought his father wouldn't be on his side, wouldn't go to bat for him, wouldn't support him. Justin was reeling from the shock of it, head to heart. "If you had found out Mom was sick early on in your relationship, do you expect me to believe you would have walked away from her? That you wouldn't have put your own life on the line for hers?"

Michael looked haggard. "I'm your father. You must understand that I have to put you first. I know how safe most transplant surgeries are, but I also know there are risks—and that not every donor comes out on the safe side of those risks."

Of course his dad couldn't answer Justin's question. And he didn't need to, because they both knew the answer: Had Lisa Morrison needed a kidney, his father would have cut out his own to give to her with his own hands if it had come to that.

"Taylor loves you," Justin told his father. "And she loved Mom." His voice felt like it was going to break, and he had to pause. "You know if Mom was here, she wouldn't stand in my way. Even if she was scared.

Even if she didn't like my choice. She would stand beside me, and Taylor, no matter what. No matter the risks."

"Your mother was the better of the two of us." His father's words were raw and full of pain. "And she *isn't* here." He rubbed his hand over his eyes, leaving it there as he said, "I can't stop thinking about how much she would have loved to see Drew get married. To think that you want to walk into a hospital and let them put you under, let them cut you open and take out one of your kidneys..."

His shoulders began to shake, and though Justin was still angry, it didn't diminish how much he loved his father. Justin put his arms around him and held him while he cried.

It was a long while before his dad could pull himself together. Stepping back, he said, "I don't think I'm making much sense tonight."

"I know this first wedding among us kids is hard without Mom." Justin's jaw was no longer clenched with anger, though frustration still rode him. "But we're all here for you. And for each other. That isn't going to change." Surely his father would come around once he had more time to see Justin's point of view? "Why don't we head back inside? We can talk more tomorrow."

"I should probably take a few more minutes alone.

You go ahead."

Justin hated leaving things on such an uncertain note. But while he wasn't going to push any further tonight, he also needed his dad to know one last thing. "Mom always said I got my stubbornness from you. She was right—I'm not going to change my mind on this. And I know it's going to be hard to change yours. But I'm not going to stop trying. Because the one thing I know for sure is that Taylor would never, no matter how badly she needs help, let me give her a kidney if you weren't on board."

"I'm sorry, Justin." His father sounded beaten down as far as a man could go. "I can't give you my blessing. Not tonight." He looked haggard as he admitted, "Maybe not ever."

Until that moment, Justin had been absolutely certain that he would be a match and Taylor would agree to the transplant and they would all live happily ever after. But for the first time, Justin felt fear take hold inside of him. Fear that he wouldn't be able to help her the way he wanted to. Fear that no other donor would step forward in time.

He heard Taylor's voice a beat before she poked her head around the row of grapevines. "There you both are. Everyone is wondering where you disappeared to." Her voice was deliberately light. She walked up to his father and pressed a kiss to his cheek.

"I can't believe I haven't had a chance to say hello to you all night. It's so nice to see you again."

"And I haven't had a chance to congratulate you both on your engagement." Drew and Ashley had asked everyone to raise a glass to them during dinner, but though Michael had joined in with everyone else, Justin hadn't been convinced his father's heart was in it.

He wasn't convinced now either.

Hating how uncertain, how fragile Taylor looked as she stood before his father, Justin put his arm around her and pulled her close. "You must be exhausted from our all-nighter. We should head home and get some much-needed sleep."

She sent his father an apologetic look as she explained, "A couple staying at my B&B had car trouble in Calistoga last night. Justin and I went to help and weren't able to make it back until early this morning."

"It sounds like an awful lot of work, running your B&B," Justin's father said. "Are you sure you're up to it?"

Justin watched as Taylor's shoulders instinctively went back. "Oh yes, I'm sure."

"It's just that Justin told all of us about your diagnosis," his father said, digging the hole deeper with every word. "I'm so sorry to hear it."

"Thank you for your concern." She didn't sound at all like herself. It was as though she was talking to a stranger now, rather than the man she'd treated as a surrogate father for so many years. "I have great doctors, and it's my understanding that dialysis can be a viable solution for many years if necessary." She forced her lips to curve up at the end, even though there was no accompanying light in her eyes. "Don't worry. Everything is going to be okay."

Justin felt as though a two-by-four had just slammed into his stomach. In not so many words, had Taylor just told his father than she wasn't going to let Justin donate a kidney to her? She kept saying everything was going to be okay—but how could it be if she wouldn't let him help her?

Before he could push past the ache in his gut to set everyone straight on the fact that he was going to be her donor, damn it, come hell or high water, Taylor told his father, "I really should get home for some sleep. I'm looking forward to seeing you at the wedding tomorrow." And then she tugged Justin out of the vineyard.

Ten minutes later, after saying good night to his siblings, they were back in his car and on their way home. Justin was deeply torn. On the one hand, he wanted to shield Taylor from his and his father's emotional stalemate. But on the other, he hated keeping anything from her.

Before he could get out so much as a word, however, he realized she was curled up in the passenger seat, fast asleep.

His heart turned over just from looking at her. He would never let anything happen to her.

Never.

CHAPTER TWENTY-ONE

It was the perfect day for a wedding. The sun was shining, the birds were singing, the sky was blue—and Taylor felt confident that nothing could possibly spoil Ashley and Drew's big day.

Her side had ached a bit when she woke, but she'd made sure to drink extra water and pop a couple of anti-inflammatories once she'd had breakfast, which helped.

"Wow." Justin took her breath away when he walked into her bedroom in black tie and tails. "Can I just say how glad I am that you're already wearing my ring?"

"I feel exactly the same way." His eyes held both heat and admiration as he pulled her into his arms, and his kiss was warm and sweet and deliciously sexy.

The last thing she wanted was to spoil the moment, but though they hadn't yet had a chance to discuss what had happened last night, there was no hiding from it.

"Your father doesn't mean to hurt anyone," she said softly. "He's doing what he thinks is best for you *because* he loves you. You can't be angry with him for that."

"If he could just think straight for one second and put himself in my shoes," Justin argued, "he'd change his mind and give me his support."

"What if you put yourself in *his* shoes?" This was a horribly difficult discussion to have, but she couldn't shy away from it. Not when Justin's relationship with his father was on the line, and she couldn't stand the thought of Justin holding his dad's feelings against him. "What if you're a man who has lost your wife, and then your son tells you that he's going to have major elective surgery?" There were no clear, easy answers here, no absolute right or wrong. "I can only imagine how hard it would be to feel okay with that if it were my son or daughter."

Justin was silent for several moments, long enough that she knew he was listening. Or, at the very least, *trying* to listen.

"Look," she said, "we don't have to make decisions right away. It seems to me that if all of us just let things percolate for a bit, it might help. And this way, we can put everything but Drew and Ashley on the back burner today and really enjoy ourselves at their wedding."

She knew it wasn't what he wanted, that getting everyone on board the donation train was his ultimate end game. But she also knew Justin wasn't the kind of man who held a grudge. His mother had taught her children by example to love unconditionally and to always look for the best in other people.

He didn't reply for a long moment. Finally, he said, "When Drew and Ashley are up there saying their vows, I'm going to be wishing it was you and me."

It was the most beautiful thing he could have said. "I will too."

* * *

Thank God there were tissues beneath every seat— Nicola and Marcus Sullivan, and their wedding event staff, had thought of everything.

Just seeing Ashley appear on her father's arm beneath the rose-covered arch was enough to make Taylor gasp. But when she looked at Drew and saw the tears of joy streaming down his face, there was no point in even trying to keep it together.

Everyone stood as the bride made her way down the aisle. Taylor relished having Justin's arms around her as they bore witness to true love. "Ashley is such a beautiful bride, isn't she?"

"She is," he whispered into her ear, sending thrill bumps through her. "I can't wait to see *you* coming toward me in a wedding dress."

She could so easily see herself walking down the aisle in a long, white gown, with Justin waiting for her, arms wide open.

She wouldn't walk to him—she would run.

Turning in his arms, she looped hers around his neck. "I love you."

He answered her with a kiss that almost had her forgetting they were at his brother's wedding. Fortunately, she remembered herself in time to sit down with everyone else as the vows began.

"Dearly beloved, we are gathered in beautiful Napa Valley today to celebrate the union of Ashley Emmitt and Drew Morrison."

The officiant looked like Santa Claus, with a full white beard and a big belly, which was what Ashley and Drew had told them had clinched the deal when they were interviewing people for the job. "I kept thinking he was going to stop and say ho ho ho at any second," Ashley had said at dinner last night, making them all laugh, most of all her husband-to-be, who clearly thought the sun rose and set on her.

"In the time that I have had to get to know this wonderful couple," the man said, "I have been happily surprised again and again by their generous spirit, positive outlook, and unconditional love and support for one another. But you don't have to take my word for it—they have each taken the time to write vows, which I will step aside to let them share with each other, and you all, now."

Ashley was first, her eyes big and her cheeks flushed as she held tightly to Drew's hands. "The first night I met you, your music was the most beautiful poetry I had ever heard. I knew that anyone who could create something so wonderful had to be just as wonderful himself. But I was scared. Absolutely terrified of breaking the rigid rules I'd lived by for so long, rules I swore had kept me safe. Until I realized that the person who made me feel the absolute safest— and the happiest—was you. I love you, Drew, for everything you've been, everything you are, and everything you will be. And I can't wait to keep living this adventure with you as your wife."

"Everyone thought I had it all," Drew said in a voice rough with emotion. "But until I met you, Ashley, nothing felt right. And then, suddenly, every-thing did. All because of you. You're the bravest person I know—there's nothing you won't do for someone you love. I still can hardly believe that you love me. I would move heaven and earth for you. You're my heart. My soul. My everything."

They were already in each other's arms, already kissing, by the time the officiant said, "By the power vested in me by the State of California, it is now my great honor to pronounce you husband and wife."

Taylor couldn't wait for the day when she would seal her vows to Justin with a kiss. When, she wondered, would they possibly be able to arrange their wedding amidst the demands of her B&B, his new lab in a nearby town, and her doctor visits?

It wasn't simple, but when was life ever simple? She just needed to remember that everyone had challenges and conflicts to deal with. All that mattered in the end was that they had each other.

Cheers rang out as the newly married couple made their way back down the aisle. As Taylor joined in the applause, her side twinged. It wasn't, she decided as she took a moment to assess things, much worse than the low-grade pain that tended to be her fairly constant companion these past several months.

She couldn't imagine anything worse than collapsing in the middle of the wedding festivities. Everyone in Justin's family knew about her diagnosis, but she'd hate for them to get so deep into the nitty-gritty that they'd be worried about her all the time. It would be far better for them to see her laughing and dancing, to know that she wasn't letting anything stop her from enjoying life.

Most of all, she didn't want Justin's father to see her looking anything but hearty and healthy. Michael Morrison had nothing to feel guilty about, and she was confident that she could help Justin understand that over time.

She took a deep breath of the air that held the faint scent of crushed grapes. As she put her hand in Justin's and headed into the throng to congratulate Ashley and Drew, she was pleasantly surprised to see Michael coming toward them.

She gave him a big hug, knowing it must have been incredibly hard to watch one of his children get married without his beloved wife at his side. "Ashley and Drew's vows were beautiful, weren't they?"

"They were." His voice was a little hoarse from the tears he'd shed during the ceremony. "Lisa and I wrote our own vows back before it was really the thing to do. She would have loved to have heard theirs."

Justin, who hadn't yet spoken, enfolded his father in a warm hug. Everything was going to be all right between them, Taylor was certain of it. Because if anything did happen to her, he was going to need his family more than ever...

Soon, the three of them made it to the front of the receiving line. And as Taylor hugged Ashley and Drew, though they were Justin's family and not hers, she still felt the pull of an extra strong bond.

A bond that strengthened even further when, fifteen minutes later, instead of standing to one side and chatting with the other guests while family pictures were being taken, they insisted she be included in the photographs.

"You're family, Taylor," Drew said, as though it was the most obvious thing in the world.

It really was the perfect day, not only for the bride and groom, but for her too. Dinner was delicious, and then the dance floor beckoned. The Morrison clan certainly knew how to bust a move, and it was tempting to watch from the sidelines, but Justin clearly had other ideas.

He guided them into the middle of the dance floor where the bride and groom were holding each other tight and slow-dancing despite the upbeat tempo of the music. He twirled her and dipped her and made her laugh like crazy. She'd never had so much fun, never felt so carefree and happy.

After all these years of longing to be with him, it felt so incredible to have her dream come true. Okay, so maybe it was more complicated than she'd planned, but they were managing all right so far, weren't they? Whatever happened next, they'd figure it out together.

Taylor was flushed from dancing when the DJ announced that it was time to cut the cake. She felt a little lightheaded and hoped some cake, and a glass of water, would help set her to rights.

The bride and groom were adorable as they first sliced the delicious-looking three-layer chocolate, vanilla, and red velvet cake. Drew made his new wife laugh, then blush, at whatever he whispered into her ear. They fed each other pieces of cake...then kissed off the mess they made.

"I'm so glad they found each other," Taylor said, even as she blushed at the heat currently being generated by Justin's brother and his new wife.

"I used to worry about Drew," Justin told her. "Especially once his music career took off—that's just such a crazy world. But once I met Ashley, I knew she was exactly what he needed. And I also knew I didn't need to worry about him anymore."

It was how she wanted his family to feel about her—to know that they didn't have to worry about Justin anymore because she would always take care of him. Unfortunately, her diagnosis meant they were *more* worried about him.

She sighed, and of course Justin picked right up on it. "I know what you're thinking," he said. "But you're wrong. My family knows I'm nowhere near whole without you, because you make my life better in every single way. That's why they sent me to you in St. Helena, remember?"

She laid her head against his chest. "I think I'm still just overtired from the all-nighter."

He didn't poke holes in her excuse as he stroked her hair. She'd slept well last night—she couldn't actually remember Justin carrying her to bed from the car—but she still felt as though her body was running on fumes.

Since her diagnosis, she had tried to be extra careful about eating right and getting enough rest, but it had been an absolutely crazy week. She wouldn't have wanted to give up any of the time she'd spent with Justin, nor would she have wanted to miss Drew and Ashley's wedding festivities.

"Taylor—" Maddie grabbed her hand and pulled her into the center of the dance floor, where the other single women were assembling. "It's time for the bouquet toss. And you too, Olivia," she added, ignoring her older sister's protests. "I mean, odds are that Taylor will get married first since she's already engaged and all. But you're always a dark horse, Olivia, so I suppose anything is possible."

Only Maddie could get away with saying such things to her sister. Taylor had meant to ask Olivia if there was someone special in her life, but Justin's eldest sister was a slippery one. It was almost as though she could read Taylor's mind, and every time she thought she finally had a chance to ask some gently probing questions about Olivia's love life, the other woman found a reason to escape the conversation. Olivia hadn't brought a plus-one to the wedding, but she had spent quite a bit of time smiling into her phone as she texted someone.

In any case, though Taylor was quite tall, she'd never caught a bouquet at a wedding. Then again, she thought as Justin gave her the thumbs-up, she hadn't been with Justin either. Now, she could almost feel her fingertips tingling, especially when Ashley looked straight at her and winked before turning to fling her bouquet over her head.

Taylor stood perfectly still as she watched the flowers sail through the sky as if in slow motion, heading right toward her. She lifted her hands to catch the bouquet, but it slid between her fingers...and hit her on the head.

She scrambled to grab it before it fell to the ground, and when she did, instinct took over. She lifted it above her head like a victor with her spoils, and soon, Justin was there too, spinning her around in circles while everyone laughed and cheered.

And then, as a wonderful surprise, Drew took the stage, pulling Ashley up with him. Never one for the spotlight, Drew's new bride blushed as he kissed her in front of everyone. "I've vowed never to keep secrets from you, Ash," he said, "but I hope you'll forgive me for keeping this one." He picked up a guitar. "The song is called *Beautiful*. And every word of it is from my heart to yours."

They were so wonderful together, and so in love,

that Taylor was already tearing up before Drew played a single chord. And when he did begin to sing, it was no exaggeration to say that every woman in the room wished for a love like theirs.

Warm all over in the knowledge that she and Justin already had just that, Taylor settled into the circle of his arms as they listened.

The most beautiful song I've ever heard

Is you

Your voice is the melody

Your heartbeat is the rhythm

And when you whisper, "I love you"

They're the lyrics of my dreams

You're my heart

My soul

My one true love

The most beautiful song I've ever heard

Is you

"That was incredible, wasn't it?" Taylor said to Justin once the last notes faded and everyone in the crowd was going wild, yet again, for the newlyweds.

"I'm not normally jealous of my brothers," Justin said, "but I wish I could write you a song like that."

"You've already given me everything I could ever want." She brought her mouth only a breath from his.

"You."

They might never have stopped kissing had the bride and groom not come to say good-bye before heading off to the airport to catch an overnight flight to the beaches of Thailand for their honeymoon.

By the time they'd seen the happy couple off, Taylor realized she was well and truly pooped. Justin knew her so well, thankfully, that she didn't need to say a word.

"Ready to head home?"

"It was the most magical wedding ever, but it probably is time for me to hit the sack." She couldn't wait to crawl under the covers with Justin and make some magic of their own. But by the time they said their good-byes to the rest of his family and got into his car, she could hardly keep her eyes open. "I don't want to fall asleep on you again tonight," she said, her words sounding like one huge yawn. "Promise me you'll wake me when we get back."

In lieu of a response, he reached for her hand and was lifting it to his lips when a sharp pain brought her awake with a gasp. She tugged her hand from his to press it to her side.

"Taylor." He stroked a lock of hair away from her face. "Tell me what I can do to help."

She opened her mouth to speak, but nothing came out around the agony of what felt like a knife spearing through her.

"Taylor!"

She could hear Justin yelling, knew he was trying to get her attention, but she couldn't focus on anything other than the horrible sensation of being ripped in two from the inside out...right before everything went dark.

CHAPTER TWENTY-TWO

Justin had never been so scared. Never knew he could feel like his heart was being torn from his chest.

He should call 911, but he couldn't move. Couldn't think. Could barely remember how to breathe.

A knock came at the window. Olivia was peering in at them. "Taylor, you left your purse."

The sound of his sister's voice knocked him out of his paralysis. "911." His hands felt numb, and he'd never be able to pull out his phone without fumbling it. "Call 911!" he yelled through the glass. "Taylor has passed out."

Thank God Olivia was always clear-headed, especially when the stakes were high, and a split second later, she had her phone to her ear. He could hear her telling the emergency responder that Taylor had polycystic kidney disease and had just passed out in the parking lot of Sullivan Winery.

Justin wanted to put his arms around Taylor and hold her, but he didn't dare move her. Carefully checking her pulse, he confirmed that her heartbeat was still strong, but she was dangerously pale and her breathing was shallow.

Minutes later, an ambulance siren sounded, growing louder and louder until it approached his car. "Sir, I need to examine your friend."

"Fiancée." He needed them to know that she was so much more than just a friend. She was his *everything*.

It was nearly impossible for Justin to move from Taylor's side, or to let go of her hand—he wasn't sure he would have managed it without Olivia's firm hands on his shoulders guiding him from the car.

"Could you tell us what happened, sir?"

"We had just gotten into the car when Taylor gasped and put her hand to her side. She has advanced polycystic kidney disease. She hasn't slept enough this week." Because he hadn't been taking good enough care of her. "Plus, she was dancing a lot tonight." Because he'd wanted to have fun. "She's probably dehydrated, and a cyst in her kidney might have burst."

Or worse.

God, no, he couldn't let his brain spin out into *worse*...

The lead paramedic spoke to Taylor, though she hadn't yet regained consciousness. "Taylor, we're going to move you onto a stretcher and then into an ambulance so that we can get an IV running. You're going to be feeling a whole heck of a lot better soon."

The paramedics worked as a well-oiled unit, and soon, she was in the ambulance with Justin crouched beside her, holding one of her hands. His family had gathered around the back of the vehicle by now, concern etched deeply into their faces.

Justin could barely think past the self-recriminations that were going around and around inside his head. But he needed to tell the emergency crew one important thing. "Her doctor is at Queen of the Valley in downtown Napa."

"Great," the EMT administering the IV said. "That's also the closest emergency room."

The back doors of the ambulance were just being closed when Olivia hopped up beside Justin. He'd never been so thankful in his whole life for the support of his family as he was when she put an arm around him and said, "She's going to be okay."

The sirens wailed as they sped off toward the ER.

* * *

Taylor's eyes fluttered open just as they were pulling up to the hospital. "Justin?" Her throat sounded raw. "What happened?"

He wanted to press kisses all over her face, but he couldn't risk jarring her. "You passed out after the wedding."

"I didn't want that to happen." Her words were barely above a whisper. "Tell them I'm sorry."

"No, sweetheart, you don't have anything to be sorry ab—"

A grimace of pain sent her eyes rolling back in her head and stopped his words cold. "Help her!" he pleaded. The paramedics already had the doors open and were preparing to roll the stretcher down the ramp and into the hospital.

A nurse came to take Taylor's full name, address, and doctor's name so that she could pull her file. The emergency room doctor grilled the lead paramedic, then grabbed the clipboard and began giving instructions to the rest of the medical team as they rolled her away through the restricted double doors. Everyone was completely focused, everyone knew exactly the part they had to play, and somewhere in the back of Justin's brain, he knew he should be thankful for it.

But he couldn't remember how to be thankful for *anything* right now. Not when the woman he loved was in unspeakable pain...and he couldn't do a damn thing to help her.

"I pushed her too hard." The words shook as they left his mouth, each of them loaded with self-hatred.

"Justin—"

"I should have been making sure she went to bed early. I should have made sure she didn't get dehydrated. I shouldn't have let her do so much this week, between running her business and spending time with me grape stomping and flying in balloons. But all I wanted was to be with her."

"Justin, please—"

Increasingly dark thoughts were swirling around and around inside his head. "This is all my fault."

"*Stop!*"

Justin abruptly realized his sister was standing in front of him with her hands on his shoulders, shaking him.

"I know you're upset, but blaming yourself isn't going to help anyone." Olivia's words were softly spoken but firm. "I'm sure the doctors are already getting to the bottom of what happened. They won't let anything else happen to her, Justin. You've got to believe that."

He wished he could, but this was one of those times when knowing too much about science wasn't necessarily a good thing. "There are just so many things that can go wrong. If a cyst burst, it could be bleeding out inside of her, or she could have abnormal heart valves, or dangerously high blood pressure, or kidney stones, or—

"Stop it." Olivia's voice whiplashed through his panic. "You're not doing yourself any good by running through worst-case scenarios."

Just days ago, he'd made a silent vow to hold on to faith, hope, love—no matter what. If only his vow hadn't been put to the test so damned quickly.

Grant, Drew, Ashley, Sean, Serena, Maddie, and his father all burst through the hospital's doors. "Is she okay?" Maddie looked as panicked as Justin felt.

"We don't know anything yet." Seeing his own family made him belatedly realize one more important thing. "I need to call her parents."

He stepped outside into the wine country night that had seemed so magical an hour ago. Taylor's mother picked up after only one ring. As soon as he said who he was, her reply came: "It's Taylor, isn't it?"

He'd thought he would need to be the calm one, but tonight everything was flipped inside out. More than once, his throat closed up around the words he was trying to say, while Caroline remained remarkably calm and clear-headed. After he filled her in on the scant amount he knew so far, she said she and her husband would be heading straight to the airport for the next flight to San Francisco. What's more, they were going to authorize the doctors and nurses to give Justin any and all information about Taylor's condition—and also allow him to make any crucial medical decisions on her behalf before they arrived, if necessary.

It wasn't until they hung up that he realized that

Taylor hadn't yet told her parents they were engaged. Though he'd slid the diamonds on her finger barely twenty-four hours ago, it felt like the distant past. One in which their worries had been little more than just that, with ambulance rides and emergency rooms only a faint possibility.

Until tonight, Taylor's illness had been a somewhat amorphous thing. Yes, he'd read her files, so he knew from a scientific standpoint just how ill she really was. But she'd always looked so fresh, so healthy, her skin glowing, her smile radiant, that he had been able to fool himself into thinking they had time.

More time than this.

He looked up at the moon and the stars—all of the best moments in his life had been shared with Taylor. Every sunrise sweeter because of her. Every full moon brighter. He couldn't imagine a world, or his life, without her in it.

He'd promised Taylor in the vineyard that afternoon with Drew and Ashley that he was strong enough to take whatever came, strong enough to help her with anything she needed. Somehow, some way, he needed to dig down deep and be that pillar of strength.

It wasn't until Justin's father put his hand on his shoulder that he realized he wasn't alone.

"It's like going through it all over again," his father said. "Being back in the hospital and feeling helpless.

Standing outside staring up at the night sky, trying to find hope that the stars will align so that the woman you love can turn the corner in the right direction. I never wanted you to have to go through this." His father's voice shook. "But I was wrong. You have to help Taylor. I was a fool to think I could hold on to you by losing her."

Justin wanted to run with his father's abrupt change of heart, but if his dad didn't truly mean what he'd just said, it would only hurt them all more in the end. "I know how hard it is for you to be here. You must be overwhelmed—"

"I am," his father admitted, "but that doesn't change what's right. Taylor needs you. She needs us. You said I would have done the exact same thing for your mom, and I would have. In a heartbeat, no matter the risks. If you're a match, tell the doctors you'll do it. Tell them you want to schedule the surgery as soon as humanly possible. Tell them your father demands that they make his future daughter-in-law healthy again."

Justin didn't trust himself to speak, so he simply reached for his father's hand and held it tight.

"Justin." Maddie poked her head out. "Taylor's doctor is asking for you."

Justin sprinted inside, skidding to a stop in front of Dr. Ishak. "How is she?"

"We've confirmed that a cyst inside her left kidney

burst. As you know, she's in severe pain, so we're giving her some pain medicine, and she's sleeping now. We'll need to keep her under observation for the next twenty-four hours to make sure there is no internal bleeding."

Justin could see from the expression on the doctor's face that there was more—Taylor wasn't simply going to be sent home with a prescription for pain pills and instructions to get more rest.

"Where is her kidney function?" He steeled himself for the answer.

"Barely above five percent." There was no way any doctor could put a good spin on that, not even for an anxious fiancé whose happiness was hanging in the balance. "It's a much faster progression than I had hoped for, so as soon as I think she's up for it— tomorrow afternoon, if possible—we will need to put in a port so that we can begin cleaning her blood via peritoneal dialysis."

Justin cursed, the word sharp-edged inside the sterile walls of the hospital.

"I do have some good news, however. I was off on Thursday and Friday, but after seeing Taylor, I just read through the tests results from the UC Davis transplant team. I can confidently tell you that you are a compatible donor."

In that moment, it felt as though every single wish

Justin had ever asked for had just come true. He'd never been so happy in his entire life, not even when Taylor had said *Yes!* to his marriage proposal.

He threw his arms around the doctor, who seemed no more surprised by his over-the-top joy now than she had by his cursing earlier.

"If you're still fully on board," the doctor said when he finally let her go, "and Taylor will agree to the transplant once I give her the news, I propose fast-tracking the transplant at Davis."

"I'd give Taylor my kidney in a heartbeat," he confirmed. "Now all I have to do is convince her to take it."

"I'll help you sway her," Olivia said.

"So will I." Maddie had never looked so determined.

"We all will," Grant said.

"That's for damn sure," his father agreed.

Justin had always felt lucky to be part of a big family, but never more than in this moment, when his siblings, and his father, were pledging their unwavering support not only to him, but also to the woman he loved.

Taylor was going to be okay, damn it.

The Morrisons were going to make absolutely certain of it.

CHAPTER TWENTY-THREE

The first thing Taylor saw when she woke was Justin's face.

The first thing she heard was, "I love you."

And the first thing she felt was his gentle kiss.

She smiled despite the fact that she felt as though she'd been run over by a truck.

"I love you." The words were barely a croak from her dry lips and even drier throat.

He held out a cup of water. "Just take tiny sips for now." He helped her drink when her hands were too shaky.

After Justin pushed a button to let the nurse know she was awake, a middle-aged man came in to take her vitals, then let Taylor know the doctor would be in to see her shortly.

"Have you been here all this time?" Taylor asked Justin.

"Of course." He stroked her cheek. "How do you feel?"

It was tempting to downplay how rotten she felt, the way she had for the past several months. But that's what had gotten her into this mess, wasn't it? If only she'd told Justin that she was feeling a little off before the wedding, he would have made sure she didn't overdo it—since she obviously hadn't done a great job of that herself.

"I'm sorry." He'd trusted her to know her limits—she'd promised him that she would be careful—but she'd blown it. Big-time. "So sorry that I didn't tell you I woke up in pain yesterday."

"I should have known." He looked like a man intent on sending himself to the gallows. "I've been running you ragged this week. It was already enough that you were opening your B&B, but then I had to go and steal as much time as I could with you when I should have made sure you were resting."

"I wanted to steal every second with you too," she told him. "So I won't accept your apology. Even if I'm going to insist that you accept mine." She took his hand in hers and relished his strength as she gripped it. "I know this is going to come as no surprise, but it's hard for me to admit when I need help."

"Same goes for me. If my brothers and sisters hadn't sent me to you in St. Helena, I might never have found out that you had the hots for me."

It was the perfect thing to say to make her laugh.

And even though laughing hurt, it was worth it. "So many hots," she agreed. And then, "Will you forgive me?"

"Maybe."

She raised her eyebrows, stunned by his response. *"Maybe?"*

"Has the doctor spoken to you yet about the test results from the transplant center?"

Just that quickly, she knew what he was going to say. "Oh my God." Her heart didn't know whether to race or just stop beating altogether. "You're a match, aren't you?"

"I am." He threaded his fingers through hers and held on tight. "As soon as you agree to the transplant, they're going to fast-track the surgery."

Utterly overwhelmed, she said the first thing that came to mind. "Your father—"

"Had a complete change of heart." Justin pulled out his phone. "He insisted on filming a video to prove it to you in case you have any lingering reservations about his feelings."

"A video?" She couldn't stop repeating everything, she was that stunned.

But Justin had already hit play.

"Taylor," Michael Morrison said to the camera, "you know I love you like a daughter, and I'm absolutely thrilled that you will be my daughter-in-law one day soon. I'm sorry that it took me so long to come around to the idea of Justin donating his kidney to you. Lisa would have been so upset with me for the way I've behaved—as upset as I am with myself. I would do the same thing for her or any of my kids, and I would expect nothing less than for my children to help the people they love. *Please* let Justin be your donor, Taylor. Because if anything else happens to you—" Michael Morrison visibly choked up. "Please say yes."

She could barely take it in. "I'm stunned." She didn't know what to think, what to say.

"Wait, there's more." Justin hit play on a second video, and this time it was Grant standing in front of the camera.

"The first time I met you, Taylor, I was struck by your intelligence. So I know you've got the numbers memorized on kidney transplant surgery successes and failures."

"What he's trying to say"—Maddie pushed in to share the screen with Grant—"is that we all want you to live a long and healthy life."

"And you will." This was from Drew. "But you've got to let Justin help you."

The camera panned to Sean. "And if you end up having any trouble with Justin's kidney, you can try mine next."

Olivia grabbed the phone. "Justin said we should

give you time to make your decision, but you know I'm no good at sugarcoating things, so here it is as straight as I can make it: It's time to get this transplant done, Taylor, and as far as we're concerned, there's only one right choice. Let Justin help you."

Justin turned off his phone when he realized she was crying. He put his arms around her and held her gently as he said, "I told them this was a bad idea."

On the night they'd taken the trip on the Wine Train, before he'd proposed, Justin had told her that when he put his life on hold to try to find a breast cancer cure—in part because it almost felt harder to accept that his mother was really gone—he had missed out on being with the people he loved who were still there. And that it took some help from his family to finally wake up and realize he couldn't miss out on his chance at a once-in-a-lifetime love.

Now the Morrisons were helping *her* wake up and see that it wasn't enough to love Justin on only "safe" terms. She needed to love him all the way, even if it meant letting him take a huge risk for her.

She'd wanted so badly to prove that she was independent and strong. At last, she understood that sometimes the bravest thing she could do wasn't to insist on going it alone—but to let the people she loved be strong for her. Just as she would have stepped up without hesitation to be strong for them.

Fear had made her hold on too tight, the way her parents had always held on too tightly to her. But if Taylor really wanted love to flourish, she needed to let go and trust.

The love she and Justin shared truly was the most rare and precious thing in the world. So she would fight for it, against any and all odds.

Taylor could barely speak around her tears, but she knew she needed to get the word out. *"Yes."*

"Yes, my family stuck their noses in where they didn't belong? Or…yes, you'll let me be your donor?"

She let her decision settle down deep inside of her, into all the places that were still afraid, but that she wouldn't let triumph over hope. "I want your kidney, Justin."

"You've just made me the happiest man alive."

"Most guys say that after a wedding proposal," she said in a teasing voice, "not when they've just been told that one of their kidneys is going to be surgically removed from their body."

"I've already got the girl." He ran his thumb over her engagement ring. "Now I know I'm going to get to keep her. And," he added with a grin, "I forgive you now."

She was laughing when the door opened and her mother and father rushed into her room. "Oh, honey!" Her parents hugged her for several long moments.

"We've been praying for good news every single second since Justin called."

"Then you're both going to be really happy to hear that Justin is a match. And," Taylor added, knowing she couldn't keep them in even the slightest suspense, "I've decided to go ahead with the transplant."

As her mother pulled her in for another hug, Justin said, "We have one more piece of good news."

"Tell us." Her parents looked as though they hardly dared believe there could be better news than hearing that their daughter would be getting a live kidney transplant.

Justin threaded his fingers through hers before they said, as one voice, "We're engaged."

Her mother's mouth fell open. "Oh my…" She finally looked down to see the rings on their fingers. "After all this time…"

"You've barely started dating," her father began, looking as suspicious of Justin as Taylor knew Justin would one day be with any man who wanted to marry one of their daughters.

"I love your daughter, Mr. Cardenes," Justin said. "I love her with all my heart, and I always have. I know our engagement might seem quick, but—"

"Eight years!" Her mother elbowed her husband. "That's how long they've been friends. And he's giving your daughter a kidney, for Pete's sake! What more could you possibly ask from a future son-in-law?"

But Anthony Cardenes's face remained stern, his gaze unwavering and intense as he stared at Justin.

"Dad." Taylor squeezed her father's hand. "You've taken such good care of me my entire life. Both you and Mom have. And now—"

"Now you want us to let you go," he finished for her.

"No." She shook her head. "I'm always going to be there for you when you need me, just like you've always been there for me. But I hope you can see that I want Justin to be my partner in everything I do from now on." She turned to Justin and smiled. "You're the best partner I've ever had, right from our first bio lab at Stanford."

Taylor's father looked between the two of them, then finally gave a little nod. "I'm afraid I haven't gotten the chance to know you as well as I would like, Justin, but I've always trusted my daughter." His lips curved up ever so slightly at the corners as he held out his hand. "You have my blessing."

Dr. Ishak walked in on the tail end of their hand-shake. "Oh good, everyone's here. Hello, Caroline, it's nice to see you again." Taylor's mother had come to several appointments in the early weeks after Taylor's diagnosis. "And you must be Taylor's father, Antho-ny." After they shook hands, the doctor smiled at

Justin, then turned to give Taylor her full attention.

"Has Justin given you the news?"

"He has." Taylor still had butterflies in her stomach at what she was agreeing to, but that was no excuse not to be brave. "I've agreed to let him be my live donor."

"I'm *very* happy to hear you say that, Taylor. In fact, in the hopes that you would, I made a few calls to the transplant center to see about getting the ball rolling."

Taylor's breath caught in her throat at how quickly plans for the transplant were thrown into motion. "How soon do they think they can perform the surgery?"

"Two weeks."

"*Thank God.*" Justin and Taylor's parents all spoke at the same time.

Taylor was still worried about everything that could go wrong. But as Justin pressed a kiss to her forehead, then tucked her in closer to him as her doctor detailed the huge number of tests and preparations that the two of them would be undergoing over the next two weeks to prepare for surgery, she truly did feel like the luckiest woman in the world.

CHAPTER TWENTY-FOUR

One week later, Justin woke with Taylor in his arms. She was usually up before him, ready and raring to greet the new day and make breakfast for her guests. This morning, however, he had a chance to hold her and take in her beauty, to marvel that she was his, and to give endless thanks.

Not, of course, that he didn't do that all day long anyway. She constantly caught him gazing at her from across the kitchen or the parlor or the garden, utterly lovestruck, thinking that he was the luckiest guy in the world. He wasn't going to apologize for his behavior, though. On the contrary, he was planning on staring at her like a lovestruck fool for the next fifty years, minimum.

"Are you staring again?" Her teasing words told him she'd likely been awake for a while.

"Can't help myself."

She was grinning when she opened her eyes. "Can you believe we're getting married today?"

His grin mirrored hers. "Best day of my life."

"You keep saying that."

"That's because it's always true."

She wound her arms around his neck and pressed her curves to his. "You know what else is true?"

"What?"

"I ache for you."

"I ache for you too, sweetheart." He covered her mouth with his and ran his hands down her shoulders and back, until they rested at her hips.

He'd been extra careful with her since she'd been released from the hospital, and she'd been careful too. She'd let him take on more responsibilities at the B&B and had also made sure to go to bed early each night so that she didn't get worn down again. Justin had arranged for five months' leave from his lab—his vacation time had added up in a big way over the past five years—and he was perfectly happy to let Grant take on the job of putting together the new lab and team in Napa. One that would be focusing not only on breast cancer research, but also on kidney disease.

Taylor's doctor had suggested they wait a week for her body to heal, and then, if she felt up to it, they could resume being intimate with each other.

Justin didn't need sex to feel close to Taylor. Smiling with her over a private joke or holding her hand already felt deeply intimate. But he couldn't deny that he also wanted her with every fiber of his being.

She rocked her hips against his, a slow and seductive press of heat and softness that made him even more desperate to have her. He wanted nothing more than to give himself up to pleasure—and to give her the release she craved—but he didn't dare do anything that might hurt her.

"We don't have to rush it," he said.

"Oh yes, we do." Putting her hands flat on his chest, she pushed herself up into a straddling position.

Though the sight of her gorgeous naked body made it all but impossible to think straight, he made himself say, "Promise me you're ready. Promise me you feel up to this."

"I'm *beyond* ready." She looked sexy, and stubborn, and determined as she said, "I agreed to wait one week—and not one second more." When his hips moved against hers entirely of their own volition, her eyes fluttered closed, and she made a happy humming sound in the back of her throat. But when she opened them again, the look on her face was pure emotion. "Before we make vows in front of our family this afternoon, I want to make vows with you in private."

"I want that too." He lifted her hands to his lips, pressing kisses to each of her fingertips, and then her palms, and then her wrists.

When he was done, she leaned down so that her

hair tickled his skin. "Have I ever told you how much I love kissing you?"

"If it's anywhere near as much as I love kissing you," he replied, their lips barely a breath away, "then I already know."

For so many years, he'd longed to know how soft her lips would be against his. To learn her taste. To hear her sighs of pleasure. In the past weeks, he'd kissed her hundreds of times. But he would never take for granted how incredible it felt when she was in his arms and he could show her just how much he loved her, the way he was now.

Shifting beneath her, he ran his mouth down from her lips to her jaw, then her neck and collarbone, and then to her breasts. She arched into him as he played over her soft skin with his lips, his tongue, and then the slightest scrape of his teeth over the aroused tips. With every kiss he gave her, he could feel her need growing.

With his hands on her hips, he moved her farther up his body, needing nothing more in that moment than to taste her desire—and to know that he was the only one who would ever make her feel this way from now on.

He heard her hands close over the posts on her bed a beat before he found her with his tongue. She was delicious, sweet, spicy—and all *his*. He loved the sounds of her pleasure, her gasps and moans, the way she begged for *moremoremore*.

One day soon, he planned to tease her by taking her to the brink, then bringing her back just before release, until her skin was slick with sweat and she was lost to everything but a fever pitch of ecstasy. But this morning, neither of them could wait another second for her breathless climax, her body shuddering as he held her right where he wanted her.

He'd planned to give her time to catch her breath, but his beautiful bride clearly had other plans as she moved back down his body. As soon as protection was dealt with, she lowered herself onto him, while she whispered, "I love you" over and over.

He would have echoed her words, but he was speechless.

Utterly bewitched.

He wanted to tell her about the million different ways she had made his life better, richer, fuller, happier, brighter. In the end, all he could manage was, "Forever."

She took his hands and pressed them to her chest, over her heart. *"Forever."* A simple vow, sealed in the most elemental way possible.

Justin would fight any battles for Taylor—all the while knowing that their love was strong enough to beat the odds. He couldn't wait to face each day with laughter, even if tears might sometimes be waiting close behind. And through it all, he knew pleasure would thread through every kiss, every caress, every breathless release.

"Next time we make love," he said in a low voice that shook with the force of his desire, "you'll be my wife."

She moved faster over him, taking him even deeper. "And you'll be my husband."

Never had two words—*wife* and *husband*—been sexier. He crushed her mouth against his as they found heaven in each other's arms while making their vows to each other in the most intimate, most beautiful way possible.

★ ★ ★

Taylor stood in front of the mirror in the upstairs bedroom an hour later, while her mother, Olivia, and Maddie fussed with her hair and makeup and dress.

"I'd ask you to stop smiling so that I can get your lip liner on right, but I know there's no chance of that happening." Maddie tossed the liner back into her makeup bag. "Fortunately, you're already glowing so much that you don't need makeup." Justin's youngest sister hugged her tightly. "I'm so thrilled you're about to become my sister."

"I am too." Olivia smiled into the mirror from behind Taylor, where she was making adjustments to the crown of flowers on her hair. "Although you've always felt like a sister."

Caroline reached for another tissue. "You're both so sweet. Your whole family is. My daughter is very lucky to have all of you."

Taylor knew this was a lot for her parents to take in so quickly—first to hear that she had been unconscious and was in the hospital, followed by her wedding one week later, and then the transplant surgery one week from now.

Olivia and Maddie each gave Taylor a kiss on the cheek. "We'll be downstairs, waiting for your grand entrance."

Alone with her mother, Taylor reached for her hands. "I'm so glad your wedding dress fits me."

"Without even one alteration," Caroline marveled. "Your father and I couldn't be prouder of you, honey. I hope you know that."

"I do, Mom. I always have."

"Everything really *is* going to be okay, isn't it?"

Both of them knew that Taylor wouldn't truly be out of the woods until after the surgery. But no amount of concern for the future could dampen her joy at marrying Justin. "I'm happy. Happier than I ever thought I could be. Especially now that you and Dad finally see what a wonderful man Justin is—and always has been."

"A mother knows when a man is in love with her daughter," Caroline said. "Justin looks at you like you're the most beautiful woman in the world. But it's more than that. He has respect for your mind, your opinions, your beliefs. And he knows exactly when to hang back and let you get on with things by yourself— and when to step in beside you. Justin didn't need to give you his kidney for us to love him. All he needed to do was love you."

Taylor threw her arms around her mother, hugging her tightly.

A knock came at the door. "Honey?" Her dad poked his head in. "Are you ready?"

Taylor took one last look in the mirror. A radiant bride smiled back at her. She was about to marry her best friend.

She'd never been more ready for anything in her life.

* * *

"My God," Justin exclaimed when Taylor appeared on the back porch of her B&B on her father's arm. "You're *beautiful*."

After so many years of holding back his feelings for Taylor, Justin wouldn't ever do it again. Not even if it meant blurting out in front of everyone that she had already blown his mind before the ceremony had even begun.

Taylor gave her father a kiss on his cheek—and then she lifted the silk skirts of her wedding dress and ran toward Justin.

He caught her and spun her in a circle, both of them laughing by the time he finally put her back on her feet in front of the fountain, where Justin's father was waiting to perform the ceremony. Michael Morrison had recently registered to become an officiant in California so that he could marry them.

"I've always known how lucky I was," Michael said, "first to have your mother's love and then to be the father of six incredible children." He reached into his pocket and withdrew a piece of paper. "Before Lisa passed away, she wrote a note for you both—and she asked me to read it on the day you married." He smiled at Justin and Taylor's matching stunned expressions. "Yes, she always knew that you two would find your way to each other."

"We all knew!" Maddie called out, making everyone laugh.

His father cleared his throat, clearly already overcome with emotion.

My darling Justin and Taylor, I can't tell you how happy I am that you have found love with each other. Justin, I remember the day you came home from college and told me you'd met Taylor. You wore your heart on your sleeve, and I knew right then and there that it would only ever beat for her. She was already your best friend, but I knew one day it was sure to become more, even if circumstances made that seem impossible at the time.

Taylor, the first time I met you, I was overwhelmed by how lucky we all were that Justin had found you. The time you and I have spent together has meant more to me than you will ever know. You truly are one of the most beautiful, gentle souls that I have ever had the privilege of calling my friend. I know that you will both cherish every moment you have together, just the way I have cherished every moment I've had with Michael.

Justin pulled Taylor close as they listened to his mother's words. His father had to stop to wipe his eyes before reading the last lines.

Whenever I think of the two of you together, it makes me smile. Thank you for giving me so much happiness. I love you both.

For several long moments, there was silence, broken only by sniffles and noses being blown.

Finally, Justin spoke. "It's like Mom is here with all of us."

"It really is," Taylor said. "I love that she was certain about us, even then."

"That was so beautiful." Caroline wiped tears from her cheeks with her husband's handkerchief. "I'm already a complete mess, and you haven't even said your vows yet."

When everyone laughed, it was the perfect segue for Justin's father to turn their focus back to the ceremony. "Taylor, would you like to begin with the vows you have written for Justin?"

The bride turned to face her groom, both of her hands in his, a smile on her lips and the light of love in her eyes. "You were my best friend from the very start. I never had as much fun with anyone else, never laughed as hard, or felt so happy with anyone but you. And yet, for so many years, I still believed I needed to keep the truth of my feelings hidden from you. Today, in front of our families, I'm so happy to finally say the words aloud and to know that I will never need to hide the truth again. Justin, your mother was right, I've loved you from the moment we met...and I will love you forever."

Though they were only halfway through their vows, Justin had to kiss her. Hearing her say *I love you* in front of everyone who mattered to them rocked him to the very core.

"Justin," his father said after giving them some time

to smooch, "it's your turn now."

After giving his father a smile—Justin felt closer to his dad than he had in years—he turned to focus every ounce of his attention on Taylor. "After growing up with a mother and father who loved each other deeply, nothing but the truest love would ever have been enough for me. From the moment I met you, I knew I would never love anyone the way I love you. I can't wait to be your partner in absolutely everything. No matter how easy or difficult, I'm always going to fight your battles, just as I know you will always fight mine. You're the only woman I've ever wanted. I would have waited a lifetime for you if I'd had to…and I will cherish your friendship, and your love, forever."

This time, Taylor was the one throwing her arms around Justin's neck and kissing him while everyone cheered and threw flower petals over them.

And when Justin looked up at the sky a short while later, he swore the clouds above formed a picture of his mother, smiling down on them for a second before the breeze blew them away to clear blue.

★ ★ ★

Taylor and Justin had agreed it would be best to postpone a tropical honeymoon until after they'd both fully recovered from surgery and Taylor's B&B and Justin's new lab had the kinks worked out. But they were able to sneak away for one perfect day and night at Safari West, a safari park set on four hundred acres in Sonoma County. They loved sleeping in a luxurious tent cabin that had been shipped in from Africa and then touring the property in a Jeep to see cheetahs, giraffes, warthogs, and wildebeests. Even better was their night of breathtakingly sexy—and romantic—lovemaking.

Now, on the day of the transplant, the staff at UC Davis were going out of their way to make them feel comfortable and at ease. It should have been the most frightening day of Taylor's life, but with their parents and siblings all there, including her brother, Austin, who had stuck around after the wedding to help out at the B&B for a couple of weeks, it felt almost like a party.

Granted, a recently married couple didn't normally get stuck with a bunch of needles and sliced open during a party...

Too soon, it was time to head into pre-op. Taylor and Justin held hands as they were hooked up to IVs on side-by-side hospital beds.

The anesthesia was slowly being administered as Justin said, "Don't be nervous."

Even as he began to swim before Taylor's eyes, he was still the most handsome man in the world. "I'm not," she promised him in a slightly slurred voice.

"How many wives get to have a piece of their husband inside of them?"

He grinned, just as she'd known he would. And even the drugs taking hold couldn't keep the wickedness—or the pure love—from his gaze as he said, "I'm all yours, Taylor. *Forever.*"

★ ★ ★

Though Justin's surgery would take place several hours before Taylor's, they had asked to share a recovery room so that she wouldn't have to wait to see him when she woke up. Logically, he understood he would have to wait several hours for her to come out of surgery—but it turned out that there was a *huge* difference between knowing something on a rational level and actually having to live through it.

As soon as he woke up from the anesthesia, Justin's family came in to keep him company. But even their deliberately cheerful chatter couldn't change the fact that time had never gone so slowly—or felt so agonizing. Once three and a half hours had passed, Justin could no longer deny that he was on the verge of losing it.

Why wasn't Taylor out of surgery yet? Had something happened to her? Was her body rejecting his kidney? Or worse?

At the thought of losing her, he swore his heart

stopped beating. Just came to a complete halt. Without Taylor...

God, no, he couldn't even imagine it. Couldn't let himself spin out into panic either, not when they were so close to what he hoped would be the end of pain and fear.

The nurses had ushered out his family so that he could rest, but how could he sleep when he was desperate for news of Taylor? He was about to reach for the call button when a nurse pushed open the door.

And wheeled Taylor inside.

Seeing that he was awake, the nurse smiled at him. "How are you feeling, Mr. Morrison?"

His body felt remarkably fine, considering he'd just come out of surgery. But he couldn't honestly answer her question until he knew if Taylor's surgery had been a success. "How is she?"

"Your wife is doing great," she replied as though he should have expected nothing else. "She will probably sleep for the next hour or so, and then the transplant surgeon will come in and give you both the full update. There were a couple of unexpected complications during her surgery, but it was nothing the transplant team couldn't handle—and nothing that should have either of you the least bit worried. Now, why don't you try to get some rest?"

But he didn't want to miss the moment when Taylor woke up. Thankfully, the nurse put their hospital beds directly beside each other. Scooting to the edge of his, he reached across for Taylor's hand, relieved to feel how warm it was.

Somehow, he managed to keep his eyes open for long enough to see her eyelids flutter open—and a smile curve her lips.

She didn't speak, but she didn't need to.

The love in her eyes told him everything he needed to hear.

EPILOGUE

Six weeks later…

Their doctors' orders were crystal clear: After being sent home from the transplant center with matching five-inch scars, Taylor and Justin were supposed to take it easy to ensure the best possible recovery. They were strictly forbidden to lift anything heavier than ten pounds. They needed to eat nourishing food filled with vitamins. And getting eight hours of sleep every night was imperative.

Only, after six weeks of good behavior, it was getting harder and harder for Taylor to fall asleep at night. Of course she loved how Justin held her in his arms, stroking her hair as he coaxed her to fall asleep. But in some ways, that made her insomnia worse—she longed for him to stroke more than just her hair. Maybe she was being melodramatic, but she swore her skin actually *ached* for his touch.

Tonight was the first night her B&B was empty

since she had opened for business. It would fill up tomorrow afternoon, but for one night, she had Justin all to herself, with no chance of anyone interrupting them. And she was bound and determined to make the most of every second with her husband.

She looked at herself in the mirror one last time, making sure everything was in place, before she headed out of her bedroom, picking up the box on the kitchen counter on her way out to the garden.

Justin was trimming the lavender plants around the edges of her garden, and the scent was heady. Nowhere near as heady, however, as the sight of the man she loved working in the fading sunlight with no shirt on and a pair of jeans slung low on his hips.

God, he was gorgeous. And even though it was still hard to believe—all hers.

Finally, he spotted her, doing a double take and nearly dropping his shears. "Taylor?"

Gratified at the way he barely got out her name, she continued to make her way across the garden to him, only pausing to put the box on the table beneath the pergola. "I was thinking it would be nice to take a break and share a little treat in the garden."

"A treat?" Again, his words were hoarse. And his eyes were huge as he ran them down, then back up, her body. "You're gorgeous."

After so many years of thinking Justin would never

be interested in her, it was gratifying to know that he would always think she was beautiful, no matter what she was wearing, whether or not she had makeup on, or had even brushed her hair. But that didn't mean it wasn't fun to knock his socks off from time to time.

Earlier in the week, she'd gone into the lingerie shop on Main Street and made a purchase. Her cheeks had flamed the entire time—the woman ringing her up had to know what her intentions were for something so sheer, so daring. But a few moments of embarrassment in front of a stranger were well worth it if it meant she could convince Justin that their convalescence should be nothing more than a distant memory.

"So are you," she said, her voice husky at the thought of all the delicious things she wanted to do to him.

She took the shears from his hands and put them down, then slid her fingers through his and led him over to the outdoor table. Once there, she all but pushed him onto the cushioned seat, then climbed onto his lap so that she was straddling him.

Quickly, she reached for the box and opened it up. "Doughnut?" She held up the enormous chocolate confection, not waiting for his response before lifting it to her lips and taking a bite.

Mmmm, it was good, the perfect hit of sugar, the only "bad" thing she'd had to eat in weeks. But it was *so* much better when Justin threaded one hand into her hair, then pulled her mouth down to his and licked the chocolate off her lips.

"Want another bite?" Her head was spinning when he finally let her mouth go, and not from the sugar rush. This rush was *all* Justin.

"Hell yes. But not of the doughnut." He put it back in the box. "You're the only treat I want." His free hand slid over her hips to pull her closer, and she moaned softly at the feel of him between her thighs. "I've been counting the days. Six weeks is a hell of a long time."

"Too long," she agreed as she tried to get even closer. "What do you suggest we do about it?"

"Funny you should ask," he said, his eyes lit with a wicked gleam. "Because I've had a fantasy ever since the day you first brought me out into this garden."

"Tell me more." It was one of her favorite games, where they told each other one of their fantasies and then made it come true.

"It's more of a show and tell," he replied. "First, I show you how much I adore you...and then you tell me you love me too."

"I love you." She whispered the words against his lips before kissing him to prove just how much she meant it.

Both of them were gasping for air by the time he

said, "I haven't adored you yet."

"Yes, you have. Every day, every hour, every second."

"True." He dropped his hand from her hair to the lacing at the back of her nearly sheer corset. "I hope you're up for more."

"Alway—" But she couldn't get the full word out, not when he'd managed to unlace the corset in record time and her breasts were springing free, right into his waiting mouth.

This time, she was the one holding on to his hair as she writhed over him. She couldn't keep from moving against him, the sheer lace of her panties scraping his jeans over her skin in the most delicious way.

He lifted his lips from her skin, her breasts as sensitive and aroused as they'd ever been. "Come for me." He brought both hands to her hips and rocked her even more firmly against him. "Just like this."

She'd never imagined doing anything this naughty outside of the privacy of their cottage, but it turned out that outdoor sex was *amazing*. She knew no one was going to walk in on them in her backyard, but even the barest hint that they might get caught ratcheted the heat between them even higher.

His lips closed over the taut peak of one breast at the same moment that he shifted his hips up into hers. He knew exactly how to touch her, exactly how to give her pleasure unlike any other. And after a month and a half of having to stop at kisses, she was primed and ready to go off like a rocket.

His name fell from her lips again and again as pleasure ricocheted through her. She'd only just begun to recover from the sheer bliss of her release—while foggily wondering if the neighbors might have heard her cry out—when Justin lifted her off his lap, just enough that he could unzip his jeans. She finally came out of her haze when she heard him rip open, then quickly slide on, protection.

She couldn't wait to have him inside of her again—but when she was poised above him, they both stopped to stare into each other's eyes.

"I love you, Taylor."

The sweet shock of his hard heat moving into her took away any response she might have made. She'd thought she wanted to take him fast and hard, but it turned out that devastatingly slow and sensuous was exactly right for their first time together after so long. They teased each other past the point of no return, and if she'd thought her first climax was explosive…it had *nothing* on the fireworks they created holding each other tight, staring into each other's eyes, and gasping out each other's names, the neighbors completely forgotten.

For several minutes afterward, neither of them

spoke, they simply held each other. "Who do you think will fall in love next?" When Justin blinked at her as he tried to make sense of her non sequitur, she explained, "Out of your siblings. I mean, Maddie is so much fun and so talented. And Grant is a heck of a catch. But then there's Olivia, who might already be secretly in love, for all we know."

"You don't really expect me to answer now, do you? Because all I can think about is heading back to the cottage and telling you another one of my fantasies."

"Sounds good to me," she said, a little shiver going through her at his sexy words. But she didn't get up off his lap. "I just hope they're lucky enough to find what we have." She looked down at the healing scars on their abdomens. "Minus a couple of these."

At which point, Justin decided to chuck in plans to head back to the cottage, laid her on the nearby chaise longue, and kissed her, scars and all, until she forgot about anyone but him.

★ ★ ★ ★ ★

For news on Bella Andre's upcoming books, sign up for Bella Andre's New Release Newsletter:

BellaAndre.com/Newsletter

ABOUT THE AUTHOR

Having sold more than 6 million books, Bella Andre's novels have been #1 bestsellers around the world and have appeared on the *New York Times* and *USA Today* bestseller lists 65 times. She has been the #1 Ranked Author on a top 10 list that included Nora Roberts, JK Rowling, James Patterson and Steven King, and Publishers Weekly named Oak Press (the publishing company she created to publish her own books) the Fastest-Growing Independent Publisher in the US. After signing a groundbreaking 7-figure print-only deal with Harlequin MIRA, Bella's "The Sullivans" series has been released in paperback in the US, Canada, and Australia.

Known for "sensual, empowered stories enveloped in heady romance" (Publishers Weekly), her books have been Cosmopolitan Magazine "Red Hot Reads" twice and have been translated into ten languages. Winner of the Award of Excellence, The Washington Post called her "One of the top writers in America" and she has been featured by Entertainment Weekly, NPR, USA Today, Forbes, The Wall Street Journal, and TIME Magazine. A graduate of Stanford University, she has given keynote speeches at publishing conferences from Copenhagen to Berlin to San Francisco, including a standing-room-only keynote at Book Expo America in New York City.

Bella also writes the *New York Times* bestselling "Four Weddings and a Fiasco" series as Lucy Kevin. Her sweet contemporary romances also include the USA Today bestselling Walker Island series written as Lucy Kevin.

If not behind her computer, you can find her reading her favorite authors, hiking, swimming or laughing. Married with two children, Bella splits her time between the Northern California wine country and a 100 year old log cabin in the Adirondacks.

For a complete listing of books, as well as excerpts and contests, and to connect with Bella:

Sign up for Bella's newsletter:
BellaAndre.com/Newsletter

Visit Bella's website at:
www.BellaAndre.com

Follow Bella on Twitter at:
twitter.com/bellaandre

Join Bella on Facebook at:
facebook.com/bellaandrefans

Follow Bella on Instagram:
instagram.com/bellaandrebooks

94130675R00188